To Oliver,

Best wish

Paul Mullins

Leah and the Waiting Game

Paul Mullins

Illustrated by Steve Brookes
footydezigns@gmail.com

Dedication

To those who believed in the Dragons

Acknowledgements

Football is my passion and once 'Leah and the Football Dragons' had been published as a paperback and people expressed the desire to buy it, I revisited the two other finished books I had – 'Amy Pineapple' and 'Another Slice of Amy Pineapple' and decided at that time that 'Amy' wasn't quite ready to be released. Even after a re-read I felt I have to develop as a better writer before I would be happy to get that into print.

So, one Sunday evening, with a spare hour or two on my hands, logic directed me to map out a follow up to 'Leah' and to see what happened to her after her relative success with Deadtail Dragons.

So many people spurred me on to write this; people at work who bought copies of LATFD (whether they wanted to or not haha), people who gave five star reviews on Amazon and people who listened to my ideas, my worries and my doubts and kept me going during 'The Waiting Game'.

Many of those mentioned in the acknowledgements of LATFD would appear again here but there are others that are worthy of a mention.

To Charlie, who I have known the best part of thirty years now and, at a football match in which his daughter played, told me to go and get some copies of 'Leah' out of the car and walked round the beer garden of the 'Shrewsbury Arms' in Albrighton and persuaded nine parents to part with cash to buy the book.

To Lee, Steven and Donna who bought bulk copies for their children's teams – The Meteors at Milford Athletic Football Club, Chasetown FC Colts and Bayston Hill Juniors respectively.

To Mervyn and Richard, for directing me along the right paths to keeping accurate records for the taxman.

To Lauren and Jennie, for listening to my random rumblings on Facebook about what to do with 'Leah' in this story.

To Steve Brookes at Footy Dezigns, for the illustrations in 'Leah and the Waiting Game' – check out their website footydezigns.co.uk for some of the other things they do.

To Elizabeth, Jess, Louise and Nick for painstakingly proof-reading the book (so it's their fault if any typos have slipped through!)

To @CastlecroftRngr on twitter for the continued publicity.

To 'The Guardian' newspaper for reviewing 'Leah and the Football Dragons' during the 2014 World Cup – their article remains the biggest source of traffic to my website.

And finally – and most importantly to you – if you are reading this, chances are you read 'Leah and the Football Dragons' too. I am proud but humbled by it all.

Chapter 1

When Jeff Helmshore played football "back in the olden days" as Leah would cheekily say, football boots were black and goalkeepers wore green football jerseys.

Now, every time a new season begun, when Jeff took Leah shopping for new football equipment he found it amazing at the dazzling array of colours available.

Leah wanted to pick her boots for the new season based on the colour. Her dad, naturally, wanted her to pick boots according to the quality (and the price of course)!

Three of Leah's teammates at Marshbrook Maids had already text her to show her that they were wearing totally white boots in the new season, two were wearing red, two fluorescent green and one girl was wearing gold. There were also girls who wore boots that had two colours on them but those would take even longer to describe!

Leah picked a pair of gold ones off the shelf.

"I'm not good enough to wear gold," she said quietly to herself, putting them back, before looking across at the silver ones adjacent to them. "Nah, not those either."

"If you are like your mother, Leah, you'll need a pair of boots to go with every combination of dress and handbag you've got! At least with Marshbrook's kit, you are wearing either red or yellow!" said her Dad.

"I don't have the handbag problem either, Dad. You can't run around a football pitch with a handbag!"

"My grandmother," Jeff stated, trying not to laugh at Leah's comment, "used to make us close our eyes when we bought new shoes. How they fit is more important than how they look."

Leah's facial expression quite clearly said, 'Whatever!' as she temporarily looked away from the rows of boots to glare at her Dad. She wasn't quite a teenager but by the end of that season she would be and was showing some of those characteristics already.

Eventually, her eyes took a shine to a pair of pink and white boots with the black logo of the manufacturer on each outstep. The blades underneath the boot were pink ("They were screw-in studs when I played," said Jeff) and the laces were white ("Totally impractical colour," he grumbled).

He may have moaned at the colour but he wasn't about to complain at the price – as a bright red tag said '55% off these boots this weekend only.'

Leah suspected that showing him the price tag would win him over!

As parents do though, he insisted Leah tried them on in the shop.

She couldn't quite grasp the reason why. The shop had carpet, not grass, there was no ball to test them on, and she was currently wearing a pair of white ankle socks which were so thin compared with her thick red football socks.

Nevertheless she obliged dutifully.

(She didn't dare complain about the wrong type of socks, as her Dad had quite clearly told her to put her football socks into the car before they travelled.)

The new season for Marshbrook Maids was just a few weeks away, which gave her just about enough time to get used to her new boots.

During her training sessions through the pre-season weeks over the summer, she had been wearing the boots she had worn during her time with Deadtail Dragons.

Like the Dragons' clubhouse and general facilities, Leah's boots had seen better days! The material was scuffed at the front of the boot, with the colour peeling away, the heels were raggedy and where the laces went through the plastic eyes of the boot, they barely tightened up enough to keep them on her feet.

Her debut for the Maidens had almost been a dream come true. In the dying seconds of the game, she had a chance to score the winning goal, until her hair, which had been growing back bit by bit, got in the way of her eyes and she misdirected her header nowhere near the goal!

Her hair was not exactly back to normal now. It seemed to have a mind of its own and certain strands were growing longer than others and every morning before school she could almost guarantee waking up with bed hair!

More often than not, when playing football especially, she plonked an Alice band on her head or a bandana headband, red if they were wearing their first choice kit and black if they were in the yellow (as all the yellow ones she had seen online looked like swimming caps when placed on the head).

The chance Leah had to score the goal had disappointed her manager Annabel Davies. So, Leah sat out the last couple of games of the season on the substitutes' bench with only a few minutes on the pitch in each game.

Miss Davies also made Leah play in a position she didn't particularly enjoy playing, as if she was being punished for her wasted opportunity.

Leah had been told regularly by her Dad that days like that would come. It was just that up until then, she had played every game for the school team, scoring plenty of goals each time she took to the field and it was only when playing for the Dragons that it got a little bit harder, not helped by the fact that her Dragons' teammates were generally as useless as chocolate football boots with liquorice laces.

The only Dragons player that could get into most boys teams in the league was the goalkeeper Luke Petty, Leah's boyfriend.

Luke had been spotted by scouts whilst playing for Deadtail Dragons during the King Charles' Tournament at the end of the previous season and as a result signed a schoolboy contract with a team in the Premier League. This meant he was working very hard after school and at weekends with professional coaches to try and become a better player.

He'd had a bit of a growth spurt too and was beginning to look more like a goalkeeper in height and build. When Leah had first met him, Luke was the smallest boy in the team and she was quite puzzled why the smallest player was the goalkeeper.

That was, until she had seen how agile he was. His manager Harry Wagstaff had given Luke the nickname 'Kitten' after a legendary goalkeeper nicknamed 'The Cat' from a time even before Leah's Dad was a little boy!

The professional training meant Luke and Leah saw each other a lot less than they would've liked, but they got to the cinema as often as they could and still had the occasional kick about in the park to improve their shooting and saving skills between two trees almost perfectly lined up to be goal posts.

Even at his young age – a few weeks short of his 13th birthday – Luke was being talked about in whispered voices as "being good enough to play for England." Something Leah herself was still hoping to achieve by progressing at Marshbrook and hopefully getting noticed by teams like Arsenal, Liverpool or Birmingham City Ladies.

In truth though, Leah was finding it a struggle to get into the team at Marshbrook and knew she would have to try harder to make that breakthrough.

At least she could hope that the new season would be a new opportunity and she had to try and get into the starting team for the first match, impress Annabel and keep her place from thereon.

Within a few days of wearing her new boots, she had perfected a demon curling free kick that even Luke was struggling to save and she was brimming with confidence that she would manage to convince her manager that it was a useful weapon during their matches.

She had also set her all-time 'keepy-uppy' record, beating her previous best by eighteen which Luke had recorded on his tablet and was going to upload it onto YouTube until Leah's Mum intervened and said 'no'.

One Thursday evening at training, Leah set up six balls all around thirty centimetres apart and with almost 100% accuracy, curled each ball no more than a few centimetres inside the post and crossbar – an almost perfect free-kick out of the reach of just about any goalkeeper at any level.

"Very impressive!" Annabel said, nodding her head in approval. "That will be useful in matches."

"Thanks, boss."

"Did you work on your fitness over the summer though? Too much chocolate, by the looks of things," patting her on what was actually already a very flat stomach. "The one thing that let you down last season was you usually looked languid and lethargic."

Leah's face fell.

"I'm saying it to help you," Annabel re-assured her, putting an arm around her shoulder. "You've never played at this level before. You are used to being the best player in your team. But, this is at least two standards higher than you have ever played at."

Leah nodded.

"You are no longer the best player," Annabel continued. "You will have to work extremely hard now to get a place and even harder to keep it."

"I know, boss," Leah said. "Luke's been helping me. I've discovered muscles in my legs I didn't know existed before Luke got called into the Academy."

Annabel smiled. "Keep it up. It's all you can do. Make Daisy and Charlotte look over their shoulders and make them worry that you will take their place in the team."

"Yes, boss!"

Daisy Ferguson and Charlotte Thornton were contrasting players. Daisy was strong on the ball, could hold off defenders and unselfishly bring other players into the game.

Charlotte was lazy but knew how to score goals. She didn't justify being in the team on how hard she worked, but purely on how many times she found the net.

Leah grabbed another ball and tried to curl it into the same corner as before but this time it made a pinging noise as it hit the top of the crossbar and went behind the goal. Leah trudged off with sunken shoulders to retrieve the ball, holding her stomach and wondering why Annabel had questioned her fitness.

The other girls had long since gone in to get changed to go home, but Leah was in a determined mood. She placed two balls on the ground, about ten metres apart, and did twenty shuttle sprints between them.

After the twentieth, she moved one of the balls a further ten metres or so away, doing twenty more sprints between the two balls, running faster and faster each time until she ran out of breath.

It was a couple of days before the local league issued the fixtures for the new season and Annabel texted all the parents to tell them to check their emails as she had just sent all the details over.

Leah sprinted up the stairs – a little out of breath, to be honest – when her Dad called her and Jeff opened his email account to see one from A. Davies among the hundreds of spam emails, mainly about uPVC windows and money Jeff had 'won' in an overseas lottery.

Marshbrook Maids had won just about enough games last season to stay in the division and avoided relegation to a lower league.

Leah was quite grateful for that. She was more than aware that if Marshbrook had missed out by a few points that she might get blamed for the chance she missed against Amberlake Angels.

Thankfully though, the draw had been enough to make sure they were safe in the league and didn't need to win either of their remaining two matches. That gave Annabel a bit more flexibility to try out new players and gave Leah that slight chance in the first team.

The email stated there had been a restructure of the local leagues to reduce travelling. That meant there were five teams in the league that Marshbrook had played before and six new teams in the twelve team league.

Leah recognised the names of Amberlake Angels, Causeway Cottagers, Parkside Pumas (against whom Leah had played the boys team Parkside Panthers), Holy Cross (she'd played the boys team of them too) and Daleside Diamonds (who Leah googled had the logo "a girl team's best friend").

She had played against Causeway and Daleside briefly last season.

The new teams were Weston Warriors, Westside Wildcats (which Leah thought could get confusing), The Poppies FC, Southsea Swallows, Robin's Wood (which immediately made Leah think of Robin Hood and his Merry Men) and Bayside Girls which, also quickly googled, were the furthest team away and, predictably, from a coastal town.

Jeff printed off the list of dates and venues to put into his wallet and Leah wrote them neatly onto the whiteboard in her Dad's study.

"Just four weeks to go then," Jeff stated.

"Yup!" Leah replied. "I'm going to get into the team this year, Dad," she declared confidently.

"I hope you do," he said, immediately wishing he had said, "of course you will" with a bit more self-belief in his daughter.

He knew that Leah had plenty of natural footballing ability, which was more than enough to get her through just about every game she had played so far in her life.

But, as Annabel had said to Leah and her parents, Jeff also knew from just three fleeting appearances for the Maidens that Leah was experiencing a whole new ball game and that there wouldn't be any more easy games for her. Her natural ability wouldn't be enough.

He repeatedly told Leah a mantra that he had been taught when he was a player – "Success is 10% inspiration and 90% perspiration. Plenty of hard work in training to get the results on the pitch."

At least with Luke on her side, Leah was getting the best education to improve, even if she did moan and cringe at times.

"Going out with you is meant to be fun, Kitten!" she complained.

"Is it not?" he retorted.

"Not overly! You can't spend every spare minute after school running up hills, doing squat thrusts, bench work, press-ups and sit-ups!"

"If I want to play for England, I have to!" Luke said, in between another set of sit-ups.

"Sport is meant to be fun!" Leah said, trying to make eye contact with Luke as his head went back and forth with each repetition of the sit-up routine.

"Nothing more fun than winning, Boy Wonder!" Luke indicated, referring to her nickname when she was the best 'boy' in the Dragons team.

"I'd rather play in a losing team than watch Marshbrook winning, if I am honest! I can't sit there every week watching all the other girls getting a game."

"All the more reason to work harder to get into the team then!"

Leah rolled her eyes, parked herself on the floor next to Luke and did a sit-up, yes, just one, while Luke was counting beyond sixty.

Before long, the first game of the season had rolled around and Miss Davies (they didn't know if she was divorced or never married) read out the first team sheet of the season, with newcomers Bayside Girls the visitors to Marshbrook's ground.

"Captain Tilly Adams, Madison Baker in goal, Abby Moore, Sarah Kemp and Eloise Milns in defence, Charlotte Black, Natasha Holmes and Zara Perry in midfield, Daisy Ferguson, Charlotte Thornton and Niamh Oliver in attack."

Leah was crestfallen. Although Annabel had complimented her a week or two earlier and criticised Daisy's shooting, she thought she had worked hard enough to be selected.

"Anna Lucas, Tegan Perkins, Rosie Ali and Leah Helmshore will be our substitutes," she continued, not once looking up from the small notepad she was holding.

The girls looked the part. Bright white numbers 2 to 11 on the backs of their brand new red shirts while Maddy Baker wore a purple goalkeeping shirt with a pale green 1 on the back.

The pitch looked immaculate too, a healthy dark green mowed in alternate light green stripes, with the white lines glistening in the morning sunshine.

Leah enjoyed the start of the season – everything brand new, even though she knew it wouldn't be long before it came round to winter with frosty or muddy pitches!

The teams lined up in their positions on the field, Tilly shook hands with the captain of Bayside, kitted out in an all fluorescent yellow kit and Maidens got the game under way.

Leah had watched football on the television for as long as she could recall, analysing positional play, applauding great pieces of skill and looking out for errors by a team, but she detested watching football when she felt she should be playing.

It probably wasn't helping her cause to get picked in the future but she really was day-dreaming away while the game was unfurling before her.

She had counted aeroplanes flying over the ground and watched a bird flying to and from a nest in a tree on the side of the ground where there wasn't a standing area.

She couldn't even go and be with her parents. When she was with Deadtail Dragons, the substitutes were able to stand with their families, but Jeff, Rose and brother Mikey were watching from seats near the halfway line in the main stand, so she couldn't even play on her Dad's phone on some of his Facebook games. (Candy Crush was her favourite).

Sitting on the substitutes' bench was a lonely business, even if she did have Anna, Tegan and Rosie for company. Leah wasn't in the mood for talking.

Her attention picked up when there was a roar from the crowd as Maddy made an excellent save to deny Bayside's number 9, a tall, skinny girl who was all arms and legs.

Leah then slumped back into her seat until the next moment of action – the referee's whistle to signify half-time in what she could only assume to be a fairly disappointing 0-0 game.

It was the waiting and the wondering that was the hardest part of being a replacement! Although she was desperate to play, she wasn't the kind of girl to think, 'I hope Daisy or Charlotte gets injured so I can take her place.'

She still did, sort of, want the team to win, though there was naturally a feeling that if they were losing then Annabel would have to try something different and Leah might get her chance.

Leah's other hope was that the Maidens race into a commanding five or six-goal lead and that Annabel would give the substitutes a chance, giving the others a rest with the game already won.

After a team talk from Annabel in the sanctuary of the changing room the second half got under way and Leah's attention pricked up again as the Bayside fans cheered noisily as the ball flew beyond the reach of Maddy into the top corner of the net.

Annabel turned round to the subs and told them all to warm up as they might be needed and Leah sprung into life and gently jogged up and down the touchline to start with, turning these into shuttle sprints back and forth to show her boss she was keen and ready.

"Leah," Annabel called, "you are coming on as sub. Make sure you are ready when the next break in play comes and I want you to play central attacker in place of Charlotte Thornton."

With a huge grin on her face, she bent down to tighten up her boot laces and was about to stand alongside Annabel ready to enter the field when Niamh struck a fierce shot from the edge of the penalty area that struck Charlotte on the bum and deflected into the corner of the net past the Bayside goalkeeper.

Leah knew what was coming next.

"Sit down again, Leah," Annabel stated. "Charlotte's scored now, so we'll leave it as it is for a bit longer and see what happens as the game progresses."

Leah had seen it so often on matches she'd seen on the television. The manager calls up a substitute, puts his arm around him, covers his mouth with his notepad so that the TV cameras don't pick up what he's saying for anyone who can lip read, the player is ready to come on, his team score and he sits down again and waits and waits and waits.

Leah wasn't particularly enjoying this happening to her though. She slumped back in her seat and knew that she would remain there as Thorny (as they called Charlotte with there being two Charlottes in the team) scored a second goal to give Maidens a 2-1 win.

Leah knew she should be happy that they had won. But, she wasn't. She wanted to play.

The full time whistle blew and the eleven players on the field celebrated in one large huddle. The four subs however moped off to the changing room carrying various items from a bag of spare footballs to the First Aid kit.

Annabel didn't have a lot to say to her players when they were all gathered back together. She saved the analysis and the advice for when they lost or drew a game. She never saw the point of talking about the game too much when they had won.

A simple "Well done! See you at training" was enough from the manager before sending the girls on their separate ways. Leah and Tegan were very quiet in the car journey home and Jeff, Rose and Mikey thought it best not to say too much either.

Chapter 2

The following Friday evening, all fifteen of the Marshbrook girls met up with Annabel at 'Bowlarama' for 'a team building bit of fun' as Annabel's text said.

"Okay Ladies," said Annabel, clapping her hands rapidly to get their attention as they stood randomly chatting and putting their bowling shoes on.

There were a couple of turned up noses at the thought of putting on shoes that other people had worn, despite the fact the lady behind the counter had sprayed them all with shoe sanitiser.

Almost immediately, and without being instructed to do so, the girls formed two thirds of a circle around their manager.

"First of all, thanks all of you for coming. If I'm honest, I didn't expect all of you to turn up!"

There was a slight murmur of surprise among the girls. Annabel had made it clear that she expected them to attend and had reminded them often enough that it would have been almost impossible to forget it was happening!

"Okay, right, well, we've booked four lanes for three games, time permitting, so this is how we're doing it."

The girls were still remarkably quiet, perhaps sensing that the quicker they listened the quicker they started.

"Game one is every girl for herself! All sixteen of us will bowl but my score won't count if I win..."

"You won't win anyway!" whispered Natasha Holmes.

"Game two, you will be paired up, the highest scorer in game one with the lowest scorer in game one etc. The pair with the highest combined total will win."

"What do we win?" asked Anna Lucas.

"It is team building," stated Annabel. "We'll all come out of this as winners!"

There were grumbles of disapproval.

"Okay, yes, there are prizes! You'll just have to wait and see."

The time ticked round to 6pm and the girls were led off to lanes 10, 11, 12 and 13. The girls almost naturally formed into three groups of four and one group of three (those who didn't superstitiously think lane 13 would be a bad one to bowl in) to which Annabel joined.

Sarah Kemp seemed to be the only one who knew how to enter the names into the computer and ended up doing all four lanes, entering Annabel's as GAFFER.

Club funds were paying for the lanes but the girls had to pay for their own drinks and sweets and they knew the fizzy drinks would soon start flowing as the intensity of competition grew.

Getting started was harder than it should have been. Although most of the girls had been bowling before, none of them were accomplished enough to know which size bowling ball was the correct one for them. In truth, they selected their ball according to its colour first and eventually they had found the right ball for them.

The venue was packed out and whichever way you looked the lanes were full of noisy children, varying from teens who were very good at bowling, down to tiny tots who had the ball carried to the metal bowling ramp by an adult before excitedly pushing it down.

In lane 10, Maddy, Niamh and Sarah were all level after frame 1 but it soon became clear why Sarah knew how to edit the names, as she got a strike in frame 3 and frame 4 to race to 76 points and her third strike in frame 6 meant a huge score of 146 with all the girls applauding when she got over 100, despite the fact that at that time poor Tilly Adams had only scored 22.

Anna Lucas made a poor start in lane 11, with just one pin from her first two balls and when she changed from a pink ball to a green one and scored three, she felt her luck had changed until again she only hit one. If nothing else, by the end of the first game

Anna had learned that the two channels either side of the lane were called gutters as her balls had invariably ended up in one or the other. Her calls to have the bumper guards put up on the sides of the lane fell on deaf ears.

Lane 11 was the closest of the four lanes though. Zara Perry led after the first frame, Abby Moore after the second, third and fourth, Eloise Milns then led for a frame before, somehow, with the change to the blue glittery ball perhaps, Anna discovered skills she didn't know she had and won with a score of 113.

Charlotte Thornton won lane 12 with 101 while poor Tilly struggled to the evening's lowest total of just 46. But, the evening was about team spirit and after just 27 points from her first fifteen bowls, it was perhaps the largest cheer of the night when she knocked down nine in one shot and the tenth pin wobbled so much that all fifteen girls (Annabel didn't join in) jumped up and down as much as they could to try to shake the floor enough to encourage the pin to tumble. It didn't.

Like Tilly, Leah wasn't having a lot of success with her bowling either. 5 and 0 was followed by 0 and 1 with an 8 and 0 meaning that she was way behind the Gaffer and Natasha Holmes, although Tegan Perkins was doing just as badly as Leah.

In frame 6, Leah was the second person of the night to miss all ten pins with both balls and, as the others had done to Tilly earlier that evening, the girls descended on Leah, circled around her and made duck wings motions with their arms and made quacking noises around her (even though Rosie Ali had to ask one of the others why they were making duck noises and Thorny explained that 0 in cricket is called "a duck").

Not surprisingly, Annabel won out of their quartet but only scored 93, still almost double Leah's 55 coming way behind everyone in her group. Even Tegan had moved well clear of Leah.

Leah was getting rather frustrated. Not only was she bowling badly but she also had a habit of breaking her bowling lane. One time, her ball rolled so slowly it didn't even make the head pin and a lane marshall had to walk down the side of the lane to push the ball out the way with a long pole. Then later, Leah knocked down three pins but one stayed lying on the lane disabling the machine from collecting all the pins to put them back into their triangular formation.

Annabel quickly jotted down all the scores into a spreadsheet on her tablet, sorted them into descending order and read out the pairs.

It was a little bit like watching the draw for the FA Cup. The lesser teams waiting to see which higher team they would get. They had already worked out that Tilly and Sarah would be paired up and trying to manually work out the others came up with all sorts of incorrect guesses.

"I reckon I'm with you."

"Nah, you'll be with her."

"Okay ladies, the pairings are: Sarah and Tilly, Anna and Leah, Rosie and Charlotte Black, Charlotte Thornton and Niamh, Zara and Tegan..."

The remaining girls were already starting to hope they weren't paired up with Annabel! At the start of the night they might have wished they had got the only adult as their partner but she hadn't exactly succeeded in game one!

She continued, "Maddy and Daisy, Anny and Natasha, Eloise and me!"

There was a scowl from Eloise but she had to "take one for the team!" as she described it.

"If I just add that to that," said Annabel, "we can see which pair would've won on our first round scores..."

"Sarah and Tilly!" said the girls in unison.

"Yes, Sarah and Tilly adds to 192 and 168 was the lowest, and all the others are around 175, so it should be exciting!"

Sarah did her bit again to edit the names for the new lane line ups, although she entered Eloise's as 'Unluck' as there weren't enough letters to put 'Unlucky' for being with Annabel.

Annabel scowled when she saw it, but she didn't know how to edit it and that's how it had to stay! Eloise didn't mind anyway. It was exactly how she felt.

Annabel looked on somewhat proudly as the girls seemed to be getting on extremely well, which was the purpose of the evening in her eyes.

As game two began, Sarah was coaching Tilly in lane 10 on how to improve her bowling technique and after four frames Tilly had actually scored more than her partner! Though, Sarah recovered with two consecutive strikes to remind everyone who the champion was! Her wild celebrations at the second strike were soon ended with extreme disappointment that she only got two pins when going for a 'turkey' of three strikes in a row.

On the same lane, Anna's score dropped dramatically, frustrated by being paired with Leah who was still doing very badly even though she did beat her first game score by a single point.

Lane 11 saw Rosie's score fall but Charlotte Black beat her own first game score, Thorny scored "only 95" despite getting three strikes throughout the game but, like Sarah coaching Tilly, Charlotte spent a lot of time helping Niamh get a higher score than her first round.

Lane 12 saw Zara get over 100 having narrowly missed out treble figures by just three pins in the first game, while Tegan did slightly worse than her opening score, as did Maddy, whose partner Daisy beat her first score by four.

Abby and Natasha were pleased to both beat their first scores, Eloise got one point less, while Annabel had a disaster, dropping from a first round score of 93 to 72 in round two, with only Leah getting a lower score among the sixteen of them. If team spirit was the name of the game, it was at Annabel's expense as the Maidens consistently taunted their manager for her poor performance!

Each pairing could just about work out their combined scores between them but remembering all the pairs was tricky and they really didn't know who had won.

They had worked out that Sarah's 103 points was the winning score and Annabel unlocked her tablet to total them up again.

"The scores on the doors..." she began.

The girls stopped slurping through their drinking straws to listen up.

"Sarah and Tilly 179, Anna and Leah 152, Charlotte Black and Rosie 173, Charlotte Thornton and Niamh 185, Zara and Tegan 171, Maddy and Daisy 164, Abby and Natasha 182 and Eloise and me 164."

Thorny couldn't believe it!

"We won! I was rubbish! How did that happen?"

The girls congregated around Thorny to high five her and Niamh.

Annabel looked at her watch. With various disruptions, there wouldn't be time to complete the third game in the time she had reserved the lanes for, so she gathered the girls together and pointed to a couple of long tables in the dining area that they could gather round if no-one beat them to it.

"Prizes after food," Annabel stated.

The girls chatted away, clearly having enjoyed themselves. Annabel could overhear much of the joyful chatter.

Sarah was naturally happy to have been top scorer twice, Tilly was smiling having almost doubled her score in her second game. Anna and Rosie were both happy to have topped 100 in one of the games, while Charlotte B had also improved.

Charlotte T and Niamh had been the second winners, Zara had topped 100, Tegan had got her first ever strike (it was the first time she had ever been but she hadn't wanted to tell anyone). Maddy, Daisy and Abby had all got a strike, while Natasha had improved. Even Leah, beating her score by that single point, felt she had achieved a little during the night.

Only Eloise seemed a bit disheartened – her score had gone down in the second game, she didn't get a strike and had to suffer being paired up with Annabel!

Annabel coughed to get their attention.

"Ahem!"

The hush descended and the girls looked up.

"The winners step forward please," instructed Annabel, holding a navy blue gym bag with mystery stuff in it.

Sarah, Thorny and Niamh stepped forward.

The rest applauded.

"Only you three?" Annabel quizzed.

"Well, yeah... you said, first game winner and winning pair."

"Ah, well, we win as a team, we lose as a team, so that makes us all winners!"

Eloise still felt like a loser but joined in the cheers as the other girls were doing so.

The gaffer reached into the bag and pulled out, one at a time, purple T shirts with the Marshbrook Maidens logo on the front and on the back 'I survived the Maidens team build' in bright white letters.

"Cheers boss!" as they pulled the shirts over their heads and Annabel lined them up for a team photo, both a front and back view. Before you could say 'upload', Annabel had tweeted the pictures to their Marshbrook Maidens twitter account and the girls got their phones out and were sharing the picture to their Facebook pages!

By the time, the respective parents had come to collect their youngsters, their Facebook timelines were full of photos from the evening.

Annabel had asked them to put their phones onto silent during the game to avoid any distractions of chatting to their other friends. But, while they were eating, most of them had put their notification sounds back on which made a tremendous racket as all the 'likes' for their photos kept pinging up – a cacophony of bells, whistles, pop songs and other random noises!

The noise level died down as the texts to say 'We're in the car park' filtered through to the girls one by one and they hugged their goodbyes and exited to their waiting parents.

Jeff was one of the last to arrive as Mikey had taken a long time to settle down to bed.

"Did either of you win?" Jeff asked as Leah and Tegan climbed into his car.

"We all won!" said Tegan.

"Haha!" laughed Jeff. "Sounds like Annabel has told you to say that!"

"Yeah," Leah chuckled. "Tee and I didn't have the highest scores but I improved my score."

"My score got worse but I did knock them all over with one ball," said Tegan.

"A strike!" informed Leah.

"Oh yeah," said Tegan, ashamedly, "I was trying to remember what it was called."

"I got a duck!" smiled Leah, who had got over it by now. "And Sarah almost got a turkey!"

"I thought you were bowling," Jeff chuckled, "not poultry farming!"

Leah rolled her eyes at her Dad's joke.

"How did you miss them all both times?" Jeff asked, the car finally pulling out of the car park behind a queue of the other Dads and Mums.

"I must have wonky arms!" Leah laughed. "Most times I got some the first time and completely missed the second time!"

"We'll have to go again, Leah, and you too Tegan if you fancy it," Jeff continued. "You'll be beating them next time."

"As long as I can use the ramp!" Leah said, smiling.

"And the bumpers!" Tegan laughed.

Chapter 3

"Dad, Mum, Mikey!" screamed Leah excitedly when her phone vibrated with the arrival of a text message from Annabel.

"What love?" her Mum enquired, as she was the only one in the house.

"I'm playing on Sunday!"

Leah showed her Mum the text.

> Hi Leah, it looks like Daisy has got the flu so won't be at training this Thursday. You will be playing in Sunday's match with Weston Warriors. Good luck. Annabel.

Leah and her Mum hugged and they did a victory dance around the kitchen, with puzzled looks on Dad and Mikey's faces as they returned and came through to investigate what the noise was.

"Dad, look!" she said, gleefully, thrusting the phone under her Dad's nose.

"Well done! Make sure you train well on Thursday and don't let Miss Davies doubt her selection."

"Yeah Dad, I will. Can I go round Luke's please and show him?"

"Of course."

Leah hot-footed it the half a mile or so round to Luke's house, where he was in the back garden throwing a tennis ball up against the wall and trying to get it to bounce off at different angles to test his reflexes at trying to catch it before it hit the ground.

"Hey Kitten!" she called.

"Hey Boy Wonder! Nice surprise!"

"Yeah, wanted to show you this!"

Leah was a lot less forceful passing the phone to Luke than she had been with her Dad.

"Great news BW!" he stated.

"Any tips to improve my game?" Leah asked.

"Just be yourself, it's all you can be," he stated. "Perform for the team, not yourself and your natural game will be good enough. You've been working hard; your boss has obviously seen that."

"Cheers Kitten."

"Where's the game?"

"Weston! You read the text just a minute ago!"

"No, I meant, where do they play?"

"Oh, I don't know to be honest."

Luke stopped his reflex practice to go into the front room with Leah where his laptop was sat beside the television.

"Weston Warriers", he said, as he typed it in.

"With an O," Leah corrected him.

"Girls Team?"

"Yeah, I assume so."

Google directed them to an attractively laid out website with a list of the sixteen children's teams that Weston had, from Under 18 down to Under 7, with more than one team in some of the age groups.

The ground was picturesque.

Behind the one goal and alongside the one length of the ground was a line of tall evergreen trees, behind the other length of the touchline was a river and behind the other goal was a railway line that bent away to follow the path of the river.

"Looks nice," Leah said.

"Does it matter what it looks like?" Luke scoffed. "You are there to score goals!"

"True," Leah said sheepishly.

"If the pitch is bumpy or flat, grass long or short, the journey there smooth or rough, you leave all that in the dressing room when you cross that white line."

"You sound like a manager!" Leah chuckled.

"Sorry, Lee." It was Luke's turn to be sheepish. "It gets force fed into me at training to leave our excuses in the dressing room. I forget sometimes that I am supposed to enjoy the game too!"

"It'll be worth it when you are a success."

Leah smiled.

Luke smiled too.

Leah had set her mobile on the table as they had gone into the living room and she could make out the funny ringtone she had chosen for when her Mum rang.

'It's your mother, pick it up, come on now, pick it u-up.'

She sprinted to get the call before it went to voicemail.

"Hey Mum!" pausing to listen before she spoke again. "Sure thing, I'll come back now."

"I'll come and watch on Sunday if you want me to," Luke stated.

"Course I do! See you then, got to dash now though because Mum's on her way to the shops with Dad and Mikey and I didn't bring my key with me."

Thursday couldn't come quickly enough. Leah was in good, confident form in training and Annabel looked on with approval.

During a little five-a-side match, Leah was running circles round her opposing defenders and scored two goals in a one-sided first half.

She was hoping to get more chances to impress her boss in the second half but about five minutes into the second period, the rain began so heavily that a couple of puddles formed on the hard ground after the driest summer for twenty years (according to the TV weathermen).

The rain fell throughout Thursday night and was still raining on Friday morning on Leah's way to school. It stopped during morning lessons, carried on again through break and dinner time, stopped again during the afternoon and was hammering down again as Leah walked home and for the remainder of the evening.

She had planned to go for a run round to Luke's house, where he would join her to run back to her house and then run home alone.

Leah looked out the window as puddles on the pavements got deeper and deeper and the drive of the house opposite was flooded due to a blocked up drain. There was a deep amount of rain covering the bottom inch or so of the car tyres.

"Good weather for ducks!" Rose said, bringing in a pile of Leah's folded clothes that she had retrieved from the tumble dryer and ironed quickly.

"Bad weather for football!" Leah replied, not looking at her Mum, her elbows planted firmly on the window sill, her cheeks crumpled up resting on her hands.

"It'll clear up by the weekend. It can't rain all the time," her Mum said cheerily, putting some of Leah's clothes into her painted chest of drawers and the other clothes on top of the chest. "Hang these up please love and come down for your tea in ten minutes."

After tea, Leah continued to count raindrops on the window pane, inventing little races between larger and smaller raindrops near the top of the pane and predicting which ones would reach the bottom of the window the quickest as she had first done when she was six or seven years old.

She worked out that the smaller drops were quicker and slowed down when joining up with other raindrops, but she didn't feel it was very scientific evidence she had concluded upon.

Eventually, she gave up on her little game and fired up the laptop to take another look at the Google Earth of Weston's ground.

The boredom of a rain-day set her mind wandering and she print screened the overhead view of the pitch, copied it into a paint programme and drew yellow circles on the pitch in the Marshbrook Maids formation, making her circle a bit bigger than the rest of the players.

She put white circles on for Weston and, with her finger, drew a curved line from her circle between Weston's circled defenders and up to the goalkeeper and drew an arrow to the goal with the words "GOAL Leah Helmshore" at the top end of the pitch near the river in bright yellow writing.

Her imagination was so wild she ran around her bedroom to celebrate her goal, ending up back at the window, where it was still raining.

Saturday morning had finally dried up the puddles and a buoyant Leah went for a morning run with Luke before a shop-till-you-drop trip round the out of town shopping centre with her Mum.

They were in the last shop before the journey home. Leah was in the changing room trying on a navy blue onesie with snowflakes on, when she could make out the distant beeping of her phone, in among all the bags surrounding her Mum's feet as she waited outside.

"Is that my phone?" Leah enquired, pulling up the zip and pulling the snug fitting onesie hood over her head.

"Yeah," her Mum called back. "It says you've got a text."

"Who off?"

"You want me to look, pet, or you want to wait?"

"Yeah, look, you know my password still don't you?"

"Yeah, Mums know everything," Rose chuckled.

There was a silence.

"Mum? Who was it?" Leah asked, opening the changing room door to give her mum a twirl in the onesie.

"Nice fit!"

"Yeah, love it! Who texted?"

"Annabel."

"Oh."

Rose passed her daughter the phone which had locked again so Leah swiped her finger over the sensor to unlock it and read the message.

"WATERLOGGED!?" she screamed.

The hubbub of the shop simmered to almost silence and a few old ladies looked the way of what they deemed was a teenager having a tantrum!

Leah slumped to the seat alongside her Mum and read the text again in full.

> *Girls, the league have just informed me that the overnight rain caused the river by Weston's ground to burst its banks. The ground is waterlogged on the far side and they have postponed the game until later in the season. We won't be training so have the weekend off. See you next Thursday. Annabel.*

Leah wanted to scream again but instead lay her head on her Mum's shoulder and pulled the onesie hood back over her head as if to hibernate from the world outside.

"Your chance will come, sweetheart," her Mum said, squeezing Leah round the waist to pull her closer and pushing back the onesie hood to kiss her on the forehead.

"I know. I was just so ready to play!"

"I know honey and you will be ready again next time it comes around."

"But, will it? Daisy will get well again and she'll go straight back in."

"Stay patient. Players will get injured, players will get ill and players will be dropped when they are out of form. You'll get a chance. Stay strong!"

"Thanks Mum."

"Get that onesie off again and we'll go and pay for it, then maybe we can get a doughnut with a cuppa?"

Leah tapped her stomach, aware of her manager's comments.

"It'll be our secret!" Rose whispered. "You can go for a run Sunday and Annabel will never know."

Rose winked at her daughter and Leah winked back before diving back into the changing room.

Chapter 4

A fortnight passed and every autumn evening after school, Leah was doing something to try and win over Annabel to get into the team.

Even against her Mum's wishes, Leah had weighed herself ("underweight if anything," according to her Mum) and had worked harder to run further and faster, managing to lose two pounds of weight.

She had even practised sit ups with the help of a YouTube video, with Mikey doing his utmost to hold down his sister's feet.

Leah had got to ten sit ups before Mikey had no strength left in his little arms and Leah's feet and legs flung up in the air with the two siblings collapsed on the floor of Leah's bedroom giggling hysterically.

At least having managed double figures (at last) she felt less embarrassed when she next met up with Luke after school and he held her feet properly as she reached fourteen repetitions at the first attempt.

Next up for Marshbrook was an away trip to Westside Wildcats. Jeff, Rose, Leah and even Mikey double and triple checked it was Westside they were playing and not the similar sounding Weston Warriors.

Jeff and Leah got into the car (it was too far for Mikey not to be fidgety all the way there) and picked up Tegan on the way, as her Dad couldn't drive.

Leah had always been brought up to see the glass as half full and retained a positive perspective as she bounced up Tegan's drive to knock the door.

Tegan had seen Leah arriving and had the door open before the bell was even rung. The two of them hugged on the front step and raced to the car, throwing Tegan's bag onto the front seat where Leah had sat before, with the two girls getting onto the back seat.

"Weston here we come!" said Tegan, confidently.

"Westside!" said Leah and Jeff in stereo!

"We've been memorising this one all week," Jeff continued. "Don't confuse us now Tegan!"

"Sorry Mr Helmshore!"

"Ready for another game sat on our bums?" Leah asked.

"Erm..." Tegan paused, nervously. "I'm... erm... playing today. Sorry, Lee."

"Huh? How come?"

"Annabel text Dad last night," Tegan explained. "Sarah's got a Christening to go to apparently."

"Aw, good for you! At least one of us has a chance to impress Miss Davies today!"

"Well done, Tegan," Jeff interjected.

"Thanks Mr H," Tegan replied. "Your chance will come soon Lee," she continued. "Annabel said that Niamh's on holiday at the end of the month."

Leah did remain positive. Just about.

Unlike versus Victoria Bay where her attention span was wayward to say the least, Leah felt more involved with this game and she hoped that her enthusiasm would maybe be picked up by Annabel.

Unfortunately for Leah though it didn't result in any minutes on the pitch during the game.

Tilly Adams had given Marshbrook the lead early on with a headed goal following a corner kick and when Zara Perry made it 2-0 only a minute or two later, Leah thought the Maidens would win easily and she might therefore get a chance.

Westside got a goal back though, before Daisy Ferguson ran the length of the field with the ball almost glued to her boot to score a superb goal to restore Marshbrook's two-goal advantage.

Annabel called Leah over and said she would be going on for a few minutes as, "there's nothing else Daisy can do in this match that could possibly beat what she has just done!"

Leah finished her warm up routine and looked up to see Tegan under-hitting a pass to Tilly and Westside were back in the game again, one goal behind at 3-2.

Annabel acted cautiously and chose to protect the lead they had and chose not to introduce Leah and instead went for the more defensive minded Anna Lucas instead of Niamh Oliver, leaving Daisy on in case they needed some "more magic."

It was a silent car on the way home.

Tegan felt guilty that her error had cost Leah the chance to play and although Leah kept assuring and re-assuring her that "these things happen" Tegan had taken it on herself that Leah would never get a chance at this rate!

But, another week soon passed by and it was back-to-back away fixtures for Marshbrook as they were due to make a longer journey, away to Robin's Wood.

Tegan got into the car, still believing that Leah had not forgiven her, stating as soon as she got in that, "Annabel dropped me again because Sarah's here this week."

Thankfully, Jeff was a patient driver as the car ground to a halt in four miles of motorway tailbacks and Leah texted Annabel (also stuck in the same traffic jam) to say that they might be a little later than planned.

Annabel was regimented that players needed to arrive an hour before the kick off, but there was no chance that was happening this time.

Jeff spotted a gap between two slow-moving caravans and was able to get off the motorway and away from the queue. The satnav found them an alternative route, arriving at Robin's Wood before anyone else, via a succession of bumpy country lanes that made Leah and Tegan both feel nauseous.

Annabel was second to arrive, but with just half an hour remaining until kick off, there were just twelve Marshbrook players there.

Annabel spoke, "Right ladies, gather round. Abby Moore and Charlotte Thornton are both stuck in traffic so I'll have to name the side now and they will have to be subs when they get here."

Leah and Tegan didn't want to assume anything, but, their gut feelings were that they were about to get an unexpected chance.

"So, Tegan, you are right back instead of Abby, and Leah you are up front instead of Charlotte. Good luck ladies!"

When she was at Deadtail Dragons, the players were responsible for taking home their own kit at full time, washing it for the next game (or not in the case of Kenny and Scott Smithson from the look of their dishevelled kit!) and wearing it for the next game.

With Marshbrook, Annabel organised the kit game by game, so, for the first time in her career with the Maidens, Leah was wearing a number in the first eleven, with Charlotte's normal number 10 shirt on her back – it made a pleasant change from 12, 14, 16 and 17 when she had been substitute previously.

Leah kicked off with Daisy and she felt in the opening minutes that everything she did was very measured and very precise. She was playing very safely; simple passes to teammates near to her to make sure she didn't get them wrong.

If anything, she was too cautious.

About ten minutes into the match, Daisy gave Leah an almighty glare and told her to, "Stop being boring! You are meant to be good!"

Leah took it to heart and tried to be more adventurous but ended up failing to make any accurate passes to her teammates. This frustrated Leah, her strike partners Daisy and Niamh, and manager Annabel!

Half-time arrived, with the score 0-0 and Leah cut a forlorn figure as she left the pitch for the interval 'words of wisdom' from her manager.

Annabel had the reputation of being hard and fair or downright angry. Leah didn't know which she was about to receive.

"Ladies," she stated calmly. "We are the better team by far. Just be a bit quicker with your passes and we'll get chances to win this. Oh, and Leah..."

"Boss?"

"Stop trying so hard! I know what you can do. Just play your natural game."

But, Leah was feeling that her natural game wasn't good enough for her teammates' standards and more looks of disgust from Daisy and Tilly resulted in Leah making more and more mistakes.

Leah got distracted and looked towards her Dad as if to ask what to do and the ball slipped under Leah's right foot into the path of a green shirted Robin's Wood player who sprinted past Tegan with ease and drilled the ball low along the ground past Maddy in goal.

While Robin's Wood's players were celebrating, Tegan sprinted up to Leah, "What are you playing at? That was easy to control!"

"Sorry!" Leah muttered.

"You made me look like I can't defend, but it was **your** error!"

"I said I was sorry!"

"Don't mess up my chance for me Leah, just because you are messing up your own chance!"

"You what!?" Leah exclaimed.

"You heard!"

Leah **had** heard. She just hadn't believed it.

She had known Tegan for years through school and never once had suggested to her that her error versus Westside had cost Leah a chance. Not on the pitch after the game, not in the car home, not by text during the week that followed.

Until now.

"**Your** error last week stopped me coming on," she spurted out, regretting it the second she spoke.

The red mist descended on Tegan and she pushed Leah away with a hand on each of Leah's shoulders. Leah stumbled back a pace.

Tegan had been sent off twice last season so her physical nature was well known. Leah's wasn't. No-one expected a retaliation, least of all Leah herself!

Leah pushed Tegan back.

Harder.

Tegan tumbled to the floor.

The referee took notice of the developing situation and dashed across, whistle in mouth, while Annabel, who had also noticed, tried to get the referee's attention to bring Charlotte on as a sub – a tactic she had wanted to do the second the ball had slipped beneath Leah's foot.

"Ref! Substitute please!" Annabel pleaded.

Her plea fell on deaf ears.

The young referee reached into his back pocket and produced a red card, showed it in the direction of Leah and pointed sternly to the touchline.

Annabel threw her hands into the air. A goal behind and a player down.

It was to get worse.

The assistant referee had been furiously waving her flag to alert the referee. He ran across, chatted to his colleague behind the privacy of their hands across their mouths, promptly ran back across to Tegan and showed her the red card too.

Meanwhile, Jeff had put his head in his hands at Leah's sending off before starting to walk round to the dressing room area to speak with Leah. At that point he hadn't spotted the second dismissal of Tegan.

Jeff didn't see the rest of the game. He was talking to a tearful, remorseful Leah in the area just outside the dressing room.

Annabel had gone to the dressing rooms too, to keep Tegan out of Leah's way until Leah had got changed and gone to her Dad.

They heard three more cheers as Robin's Wood ended the game 4-0 winners as Annabel and Tegan came out the dressing room to stand in front of Jeff and Leah.

Jeff said, "Leah, in the front of the car now! Tegan, I've sent a text to your parents. In the back of the car please!"

Both girls were looking to the floor, raising their head slightly to acknowledge comprehension of what they were told.

He turned to Annabel.

"I'll ring you once I've got these two home," he said.

"Okay," she replied. "Girls," emphasising the choice of word rather than 'ladies', "I will speak with your parents later. That is all I have to say."

Thankfully the journey home was not littered with motorway hold ups and the car was so silent that you would have heard a pin drop if Jeff had one to drop.

Jeff wasn't one for driving above the speed limit, especially when he was driving someone else's child around, but he was certainly eking out every mile per hour he could, to get home in the quickest available time.

Eventually, the car pulled into Tegan's cul-de-sac. Jeff brought the car to a stop and Tegan thanked Mr Helmshore and didn't look back towards Leah as she walked up the path.

'See you next week', 'I'll text you', 'See you at training' didn't seem appropriate conversations. So nothing was said.

Mrs Perkins was stood at the front door though and tapped Tegan on the head as she brushed past her Mum. She didn't really know what to say either, so all she did was wave "Hi" to the Helmshores, mouthing an almost apologetic "Thanks" before she closed the door.

"Dad..." Leah started.

"Not now, Lee!"

A few more silent minutes passed until they returned home and Jeff reversed onto the drive.

Leah looked towards him as if to ask for permission to speak. Permission wasn't granted.

"Straight to your room Leah please... and no privileges!"

"Yes Dad," she replied.

Leah lay face down on her bed, close to tears, but was still managing to keep them within her so far.

Her iPad was already switched off but she switched off her mobile and put it onto the bedside table next to it.

The door opened slowly but Leah remained virtually motionless as her Mum put a cold drink down on the table and lifted both devices.

"Lunch is at 2, Leah. You can come down then," Rose stated, closing the door when Leah had replied "Yes Mum" in acknowledgement.

Although it was only an hour until 2pm it felt like many, many more. It eventually rolled around though after what seemed like 'hours' of no texting, no Facebook, no television, no music.

Leah knew that accepting her punishment more quickly would mean things would return to normal. So, she had just lay there doing what all parents seem to say to their children at one point, "Think about what you have done!"

She tiptoed down the stairs as the landing clock pinged twice for the time, to see Mikey in the front room on the beanbag eating chicken nuggets while Jeff and Rose were sat at the table awaiting Leah.

She may have avoided the tears so far but one look at her Mum and Dad's disappointed faces was enough to begin the waterworks!

"I'm so sorry," she blurted out, dashing to hug her mum as she spoke.

"Eat up. We'll talk after."

Like many parents, Jeff and Rose could equally play the role of good cop, bad cop depending on the situation. It was clear to both of them that Leah had accepted her initial punishment graciously and her face quite clearly was full of remorse.

Rose looked at Leah, waiting for her to speak.

"Well..." she prompted her.

"I was rubbish... didn't play well," Leah began, downward facing.

"Look up when you talk to us!" Rose insisted.

"Tee said something about me costing her place in the team and my head said 'she cost you yours' but I said it before I realised I shouldn't have."

"And?"

Leah knew that her Mum would already know all the details but continued anyway.

"She pushed... I pushed... harder."

Leah paused.

"How do I tell her I'm sorry?" Leah questioned.

"Who?" Rose asked. "Tegan? Annabel?"

"Both! All the team! You two."

The tears fell again.

"What now?" Leah asked.

Chapter 5

It took a week for the letter to come from the local football association. It was addressed to Annabel Davies as manager but a copy was sent to the Helmshores too. It stated:

The referee at the match between Robin's Wood and Marshbrook Maids submitted his report concerning an incident in the second half between two players from the away side.

He deemed that the players concerned – Leah Helmshore of Marshbrook Maids and Tegan Perkins also of Marshbrook Maids – were involved in an incident during which both players raised their arms towards one another in what was deemed an aggressive manner by the referee and his assistant.

The officials deemed that the incident was begun by Miss Perkins and retaliated by Miss Helmshore and that both players were guilty of a sending off offence, stating that it was serious enough to be irrelevant whether the incident had occurred between opposing players or between teammates.

As a result, Miss Perkins will receive a one match suspension ruling her out of the game between Marshbrook Maids and Amberlake Angels.

Miss Helmshore will receive a three match suspension ruling her out of the games between Marshbrook Maids and Amberlake Angels, between Marshbrook Maids and Holy Cross and between The Poppies FC and Marshbrook Maids.

The committee discussed the contents of the referee's report and considered the risk of injury to Miss Perkins sufficient to make the incident of a more serious nature.

The letter went on to explain about the players having a right to appeal against the decision but when Jeff read that bit out, before Leah could say anything, he stated that they would not question the league's decision.

In the week that had followed the game, Leah and Tegan had apologised in private and were then coerced to apologise in public in front of the rest of their teammates at training.

The two of them were banned by Annabel from taking part in the training though. They were forced to sit it out and watch the others, knowing that they would be missing some games, and to add insult to injury they saw two new girls at training – a defender called Simone Ellis and a very quick goalscorer called Rita Gildesunder who would rival Daisy, Charlotte and Niamh's place in the team, let alone Leah's.

Simone Ellis scored the only goal of a 1-0 win in the game that Tegan missed against Amberlake, which neither Tegan nor Leah were allowed to go and watch – again, orders from Annabel to stay away.

Then, even when Tegan was available again to play against Holy Cross, she hadn't found anyone else to give her a lift to the game and stayed at home as Leah was asked not to attend that one either.

Leah looked on the team's website to see that Daisy Ferguson scored three goals, Charlotte Thornton four goals and Niamh Oliver three goals with Marshbrook thrashing Holy Cross 10-1.

There was no mention of the new girl in that game, but then Rita scored all six goals in a 6-3 away win at the Poppies when Niamh was on holiday – a game that Leah thought she was almost certain to have played in if she had been eligible to do so.

If it was hard enough to make an impression on her manager at the start of the season, Leah was definitely playing a waiting game now to get another chance with the Maidens.

With the ban over, Annabel permitted Leah and Tegan to watch the games again, explaining that her fear had been that their attendance would be a disruptive influence on a team that was otherwise doing well in the season.

There had been a few days of the silent treatment by Tegan to any text or Facebook message that Leah had sent her but the two girls were now talking again. They were both back among the squad for an away trip to Parkside Pumas, but neither got on the pitch.

Pumas were winning for most of the game but Charlotte Thornton scored ten minutes before the end and Niamh Oliver came on as substitute to score the winning goal. With Daisy Ferguson and Rita Gildesunder setting up the goals too, Leah spent another game looking on rather than being involved, hoping for a chance for something to happen that would give her an opportunity to play again.

Weston Warriors thrashed Marshbrook 4-1 in the next game and Leah, again, spent the whole game watching everything go on around her. She couldn't even take enjoyment from Daisy, Charlotte and Rita struggling because the three of them set up "one of the best goals ever" for Niamh in the final minute which Annabel described as a "golden lining on a very grey cloud."

"I've had enough Dad!" Leah grumbled.

"Of?"

"Waiting!"

"Oh."

"I know it's my own fault but I'm never going to get back in the Maidens' team, am I?"

"Never say never," Jeff reassured her. "But, if you want to ask around at the other teams, you know I'll support you."

"I was wondering about Southsea Swallows…"

"You know Marshbrook play them next though, don't you?"

"Yeah Dad, I know but it's one of the nearer teams and I wouldn't get into some of the teams we've played. They are bottom of the league so at least I'll have a chance of getting in the team!"

"It'll be like Deadtail all over again for you!" Jeff chuckled. "Bringing a team of misfits up to your standard, no doubt!"

The following Thursday, the two of them made their way over to the Southsea ground. It immediately felt like déjà vu of her first experience of Deadtail Dragons.

All of the 'buildings' were portacabins, there wasn't a clubhouse and the changing rooms, if they could be called that, had certainly seen better days.

Leah pictured in her mind eleven girls trying to change in there, and like a mental Tetris puzzle trying to fit all the pieces in at different angles, she certainly couldn't see how a team of teenage girls could all get in there at the same time!

"Excuse me?" Jeff enquired, calling out to a slim lady who had her back to him.

She turned round. She must have been no older than 20 with a very neat blonde hairstyle with a pony-tail hanging over one shoulder.

"Are... are you in charge here?" Jeff enquired.

"I am."

She reached out to shake Jeff's hand.

"Jeff Helmshore," he stated, "and this is Leah."

"Hi Leah. Hi Jeff. I'm Hannah."

"Are you taking on new players?" Jeff enquired.

"Yeah, we sure are. We're always on the look-out for players that can improve the team. You play for anyone at the moment, Leah?"

"Erm... yeah... I'm with Marshbrook Maids."

"And you want to step down to us? Why?"

Jeff interceded before Leah could answer.

"Leah's struggled to get in the team this year and when she had a chance she got herself sent off and she's not got back in the team since."

"I just want to play, Miss," Leah stated. "I'll do anything to get a game."

"That's true!" Jeff whispered to Leah, recalling her Deadtail Dragons days!

"Well, we only train on Thursday nights and games as you know are on Sundays. We've only got eleven players here most weeks to be honest so we barely get a team out to play."

Leah nodded.

"**But**," Hannah continued, stressing the word 'but' quite powerfully, "I'm a loyal coach. It's sad, but we lose most of our matches anyway. The girls here just want to play. So, even if you were as good as Lionel Messi, you wouldn't walk straight into the team."

Leah was still nodding, like one of those dogs you sometimes see on the parcel shelf in the back of a car.

Hannah continued, "The girls play with a smile here. I would rather pick the person who fits in well than a top player who would rock the boat."

"Yes, Miss," Leah stated politely.

"It's Hannah," she said, chuckling. "I'm not much older than the girls I manage! I'm too old to be called 'Miss'!"

Leah played with a confidence and a swagger that had been missing in her games for the Maidens and had the rest of the girls at the Swallows gulping with amazement at what she could do with a ball at her feet.

"She has to play against Marshbrook!" a chorus of voices came up from the girls at the end of the game.

"You know my ethos," Hannah stated. "We play to enjoy the game, not to win. I won't just put any player straight in."

"I don't mind," piped up Bonnie Thompson, the only striker Southsea had.

"Thank you, Bonnie, but no. If the twelve of you that are here tonight are all fit and well to play on Sunday then Leah will be the substitute."

Hannah shook Leah's hand, then Jeff's.

"Welcome aboard, Leah. Hopefully this will give you the chance you've been waiting for."

Within seconds of getting back through the front door, Leah grinning from ear to ear, Jeff was on his computer to email the league association.

As well as informing the league, he also emailed Annabel that Leah would be changing teams and Southsea turned up at Marshbrook's ground with Leah excited to have the chance to play again, having been promised to play "some or all of the second half" by Hannah.

Already, it felt strange for Leah to be walking into the away team dressing room, coming out in a yellow football shirt with a red number 12 on the back and sitting down on the opposite substitutes bench to where she had sat for most of the three months of the season so far.

Ironically, the Maidens bench was empty. Annabel spoke briefly to Leah and told her that her "timing wasn't great". Rosie Ali didn't want to play football anymore (as she had got herself a boyfriend who played rugby and she'd rather watch him) while Anna Lucas had broken a toe playing hockey for the school. Both Charlottes were away on holiday and Tegan said to her Dad that it "wouldn't be right" if she travelled to the match with Leah and Jeff – "now the opposition" – so she had decided not to bother that week!

"Oi! 'Annah!" bellowed a loud voice from behind the bench.

"Who's Anna?" thought Leah.

"Dad, you made it!" Hannah exclaimed. "This is our new player I was telling you about..."

"Leah 'Elmshore!" he stated.

"Mr Wagstaff!" shouted Leah, and couldn't resist throwing her arms around him.

"You two know each other?!" Hannah Wagstaff stated.

"We sure do! Leah – or should I call you Lee – was our star player for Deadtail last year!" he said with a sparkle in his eyes.

Leah and Harry could have talked for hours but the kick off was imminent.

"Okay, girls, gather round," Hannah began. "The team today is the same as last week, Gilly in goal, Paris, Lizzie, Sarah and Alice in defence, Terri, Becky, Kaitlyn, Katy and Jessie in midfield and Bonnie our striker."

Harry smiled at Hannah's loyalty to the team, despite the fact they knew their best player would be sitting on the reserves bench.

"The subs, yes, we have three this week!" Hannah exclaimed "We have Leah, Abi and Laura, and welcome them to all."

Leah sat down next to Abi and Laura and began talking to them. "Are you new too?" she asked.

"Hannah's our aunty," Abi said.

"Yeah, she thought two of them were on holiday this week so she kinda forced us to come along!" Laura chuckled. "We've never even played before!"

"Doubt we'll come again either," Abi said, smiling. "It's just to get us out of the house cos Mum and Dad keep arguing."

"You twins then?" Leah asked. "You don't look alike."

"Nope," Laura said, in a matter of fact way. "Sisters. I'm a September birthday, Abi's an August birthday!"

"Wow!" Leah said, raising her eyebrows in shock as Laura had spoken, not sure whether they were joking with her.

The whistle blew to start the game but it was not long before, as would have been expected, Marshbrook scored the first goal, Sarah Kemp chipping the ball over Gilly Whitbread's head from a long distance.

The goals kept on coming throughout the first half, yet Southsea – like Deadtail Dragons did before – never got demoralised. Not when Carrie Oakley made it 2-0. Not when Natasha Holmes made it 3-0. Not when Sarah Kemp got her second goal to make it 4-0.

Leah was warming up at this point, not that she could reverse a 4-0 scoreline on her own and even Marshbrook defenders Abby Moore and Eloise Milns scored in a one-sided first half to make it 6-0 at the interval.

Hannah gathered the girls round and, with a huge smile on her face, cheerily said, "Well, that's less goals than we expected, eh? There are teams in this league better than us who have let in six goals against these!"

The Swallows tried to smile. They did enjoy playing, even though losing was very much a habit for them. They enjoyed the social side of it all – going bowling, swimming together, training, having a giggle.

"Unleash Leah!" Bonnie said, "I think she has a point to prove!"

"I'm not **that** good!" Leah stated.

"Aw, but you'll have a go!" Hannah said. "Leah for erm…"

"Me," Bonnie said. "We're not going to get a shot are we?"

"No, I will," Katy Wheel chipped in. "Let's play two strikers now we've got two at the club!"

Their enthusiasm was infectious.

"That's my gal, 'Annah!" Harry said, putting his arm around Hannah and giving her an almighty hug.

Leah chuckled.

"What's ticked you, Boy Wonder?" Harry asked.

"Boss…" Leah enquired.

"Yeah?"

"Why did you call your daughter Hannah when you can't pronounce your H's?"

"It was Mrs Wagstaff! She thought it was funny when she told the nurses. Must 'ave been the laughing gas!"

The referee stopped the game to allow the change to take place. Leah stood at the half way line as Hannah held up the numbers 10 and 12 to replace Katy with Leah.

Annabel looked across approvingly at Leah, as if to say, "Good luck" but no words came out of her stern mouth.

Marshbrook quickly got possession of the ball though and before Leah even touched it, the score was 8-0, goals from Niamh Oliver and Tilly Adams.

After the ninth time the Swallows kicked off, Bonnie tapped the ball to Leah and she got the ball onto her right foot, swerved past Tilly, sprinted between Zara and Natasha and was staring Maddy in the eyes with just the goalkeeper left between her and the net.

Leah pulled back her left foot as it seemed the obvious one to use, Maddy made a slight step to her right to anticipate the shot and, almost in slow motion, everyone looked on expecting to see the ball fly past Maddy into the net or smack off the white gloves of the Maidens goalkeeper to push the ball aside.

Annabel watched.

Hannah watched.

Harry watched.

Jeff watched.

Abi and Laura didn't – they were on Facebook on their phones.

"GOAL!" shouted Hannah. "Our first one this season!"

"My first one ever!" shouted Bonnie, leaping into the air in ecstasy! "Thanks Leah!"

"You're welcome!"

She had surprised everyone, especially goalkeeper Maddy Baker, feigning as if to shoot the ball into the net but instead rolling it to Bonnie who had sneaked alongside her as she had dodged past Natasha.

"8-1!" Harry shouted down his phone, probably to Mrs Wagstaff. "Swallows got a goal!"

The excitement was short-lived though as Tilly and Rita got further goals for a 10-1 win.

The Swallows weren't bothered though.
"Milkshakes all round," said Harry. "You deserve it gals!"

Chapter 6

It wasn't long before Harry Wagstaff teamed up with his daughter to help Southsea Swallows with their training. Despite his limited success with Deadtail Dragons, he did know a thing or two about it.

With Leah, his star player back under his wings, Harry's zest for football had returned and the infectiousness of Hannah's positivity – even when losing – made him want to be involved again.

That 10-1 defeat to Marshbrook though was followed by a smaller loss (4-1) to Victoria Bay, although Leah got her first goal of the season, eleven weeks after the season had started.

The Swallows girls were enjoying training now and Leah taught them a trick or two, as well as helping their technique and skills. Leah could still perform that demon free-kick that had impressed Annabel in pre-season.

It was starting to pay off. Against Westside Wildcats, Paris, Terri, Kaitlyn and Jessie all scored their first ever goals – unfortunately for Swallows, Gilly let in eight goals and they were beaten 8-4. But, they were starting to look like a team that maybe, just maybe, could get better.

Even when they went to Robin's Wood, who the Maidens had lost 4-0 against, they played enthusiastically, scored four more goals but again lost 6-4. Leah scored two of the goals – a happier return than when she had been sent off there with Tegan.

But, that team 'form' was short-lived. The Swallows defence was as watertight as a sieve and in their next four games they let in nine, eight, seven and nine again, to be firmly rooted at the bottom of the league (not that they had ever expected to be any higher).

Every week though, since she had begun playing for the Dragons, win, lose or draw (mostly lose) Leah looked through the local free newspaper to see if there was any mention of the game and, if there was, she'd run to get a pair of scissors, walk back (as any good teacher will tell you, you don't run when holding scissors), cut the article out and stick it into a scrapbook.

"You know who we've got next week, don't you Dad?" she called out from the top of the stairs.

"Yup, Marshbrook at home," he replied. "Let's try and keep the score to under 10-0 shall we!?"

"We might score again!" Leah replied. "We have started scoring goals."

"So have the opponents! I'm not sure why Gilly needs gloves, she doesn't save many!"

"That's nasty Dad," Leah called, folding her arms across her chest and storming back into her bedroom.

Lying in her bed, she texted Tegan to see if she was going to play next week. Conveniently, Tee had a birthday party to go to in the evening and was unable to play.

"Hmmph!" grumbled Leah, putting her phone on the bedside cabinet.

The phone didn't stay there long though. First, Maddy Baker texted Leah, then Tilly Adams did, then Daisy Ferguson did. She even noticed a friends request from Rita Gildesunder on Facebook and she hadn't even really met her before.

It was a good job Leah's parents had paid for her to have a contract with unlimited texts because the phone was beeping every few seconds batting a conversation back and forward between Leah and three of her former teammates.

Leah thought it was quite strange. They certainly couldn't be trying to unsettle her before the game. No-one in their right mind would believe that Southsea had any hope of beating Marshbrook, not after the scoreline last time!

BEEP BEEP. Her phone went off again. It was Charlotte Thornton this time.

u r getting quite gd at southsea, thorny x

> *thx, lee x*

u won't beat us tho, thorny x

> *I know, lee x*

just don't stop us winning the league, thorny x

> *I doubt we will lol, lee x*

gd. make sure u don't

Leah didn't reply to that one. It wasn't signed Thorny and it certainly didn't have a kiss. Leah showed the phone to her mum.

"Sounds like they are scared love," she stated. "There's a threatening tone to that last one."

"That's what I wondered! As if we'd beat them!"

"Maybe that's not what they are scared of?" Jeff interrupted, showing Leah and Rose a snippet in the local newspaper.

'Mayor bowled over by Maidens!' stated the headline.

Marshbrook Maids are facing an interesting two weeks in their bid to get promotion out of the Midland Junior League. Mayor Lawrence visited the ground earlier this week with Football Association representatives to approve the club's facilities as acceptable for promotion.

With just two defeats all season, a win over bottom club Southsea Swallows will move the Maidens into second place with four games remaining.

Manager Annabel Davies exclusively told the Mercury, "If we win on Sunday, we will give ourselves a two point lead over Robin's Wood in third place.

"It's vital we try and win this one by a lot of goals. We play away at runaway league leaders Weston Warriors on the last day of the season and we have to try to get in a position where we only need a draw in that one to secure promotion.

"We already have scored four goals more than Robin's Wood," she continued, "so any win above six goals would give the Maidens a big advantage on goal difference and would mean that a point should be enough on the final day."

Mayor Lawrence said it would be "a major boost" for local girls' football if Marshbrook gained promotion.

"Ah!" thought Leah. "They think we're getting better, so they might not thrash us anymore!"

Leah laughed.

"I'm going to text Hannah now to see if she's seen it."

Hannah had seen it. In fact, she'd already cut it out, enlarged it on the photocopier at work and had stuck it onto the wall of the changing rooms at Southsea, with all eleven players huddled closely together on the rickety benches in the shack that they dared to call a changing room.

That was nothing compared with the hostile reception Marshbrook would receive with their facilities. It was a bitterly cold spring morning, with the early morning frost only just melted on quite a muddy pitch by the time kick off came around at 2pm.

Hannah had smuggled a very small heater into their changing rooms to keep Southsea girls warm while they got changed, but she deliberately provided nothing for Marshbrook whose players' teeth chattered as they squashed into an even tinier space in their changing room, with Maddy Baker virtually wedged against a smelly, rusty exercise bike that had been put in there that morning to make the space even more cramped.

On the wall, there was a poster that had clearly only been put there that morning. "Enjoy your promotion. Winning here is easy!" It was the only thing in the room that looked new.

Hannah squeezed into the middle of her team ready to give her team talk.

"Okay girls, we know what the newspaper said. They have come here to win and to win easily. Let them do their best! And we'll do our best to make it hard for them!"

"Go Swallows!" came the collective chant from the players.

"I thought long and hard about the team today," Hannah continued. "I always said that taking part was more important than winning, and it is..."

"Here comes a 'but'," piped up Paris Robinson.

"...but," Hannah continued, "that newspaper article, that one there," she said, pointing furiously at it, "has really, really wound me up this week! Go out there, kick some you-know-what, girls! Stop these girls winning that promotion, whatever it takes!"

"Go Hannah!" chipped in Kaitlyn Allen.

"They will expect us to defend with ten players today to try and stop them scoring, but, uh-uh," Hannah said, wagging her finger. "We fight attack with attack, we will play with three strikers and keep their defence occupied!"

"We don't have three!" quizzed Bonnie.

"We do today! Gilly in goal, Paris, Lizzie, Sarah and Alice in defence, Terri, Becky and Kaitlyn in the middle, Bonnie, Leah and Katy up front."

Katy gasped.

"Oh, and one more thing," Hannah whispered, "Leah, this is your shirt number today."

She threw Leah her yellow Swallows shirt. Leah turned it round.

"2?" she asked.

"Reverse psychology, Leah, my dear," Hannah said, still whispering. Leah half expected her to cackle like a witch mixing up a deadly potion. "The Maidens will see the team sheet, see Leah down as number 2 and will assume we've gone for a defensive formation! Then..."

BAM! Hannah slammed her hand against the enlarged newspaper article making the girls jump and the changing room shake and creak loudly.

"...Leah will return to being a striker and their minds will be messed with and we will WIN WIN WIN!"

There was a deathly silence. The girls had never seen Hannah so animated in her team talks. She was normally, "Go and enjoy it girls and have fun!" with a jolly, glee, quirky voice.

Today, it was a war cry. In Hannah's eyes, this **was** war. The question was whether her troops had enough ability to carry off the mission.

Chapter 7

There was a knock on the door of the home changing rooms as Annabel tried to alert Hannah that they were ready to hand the team list to the referee.

They walked to the referee's room, knocked on the door, waited until they could enter and gave the team sheet to the man in black, a scrawny young man who was only just old enough to officiate a match.

He gingerly peeled off the top cover of the duplicated sheets and gave the Swallows team sheet to Annabel and the Maidens team sheet to Hannah so that both managers could see the list of their opponents.

Hannah waited patiently.

"TWO?!" Annabel exclaimed.

She was normally quite reserved and poker-faced when it came to showing her emotions but this crept out and Hannah automatically smiled inside that they had gained some sort of advantage by tricking Annabel into thinking that they were going to use Leah as an extra defender.

The players walked out, lined up and shook hands with one another and the match officials like two colourful snakes passing each other in the grasslands.

Leah heard a couple of her former teammates say, "Two" with surprise in their voice as they walked past.

And, true to the number on the back of her shirt, Leah lined up in a defensive position just to the right of Paris, who was wearing three which was normally Lizzie Jones' number.

Swallows chose to kick off first after calling "Heads" when the referee tossed a rather grubby 50 pence piece into the air.

Bonnie and Katy stood over the ball and Leah stood way, way back from the play in the defensive position she was instructed to occupy.

Bonnie rolled the ball to Katy, who put her foot on top of the ball and rolled it backwards to Leah. The Maidens expected a negative piece of play from the Swallows, possibly passing it along to Paris and then along to Lizzie and were stood there watching, feet flat to the floor.

Leah took one touch of the ball and sprinted beyond Daisy Ferguson, then another to whiz past Natasha Holmes.

Before Tilly Adams and Sarah Kemp had realised what was going on, Leah had shimmied her way between them and advanced on Maddy Baker as she sprinted out from her goal line.

Katy and Bonnie had managed to keep up with Leah and one simple pass either side and Swallows would take the lead.

Expecting a pass, like last time, Maddy stood up straight ready to dive either left or right but Leah bluffed her by drawing back her right foot and poking the ball low through Maddy's legs.

She hadn't hit it with any pace though and the ball seemed to take an age to get towards the goal, allowing time, somehow, for Tilly to sprint back, stretch out a leg and hook the ball away from the goal.

Unfortunately for Tilly, it ricocheted straight off Maddy and into her own goal. Swallows were leading!

Annabel was raging on the side-line, which seemed to transmit itself into her players who suddenly self-destructed in their performance and their temperament.

Tilly and Sarah were arguing among themselves when Leah got another shot at goal which Maddy saved for a corner and then Maddy was bawling at Abby Moore when Bonnie Thompson was given the ball right in front of goal and gave Swallows an astonishing 2-0 lead!

Thankfully for Marshbrook, half-time was imminent and, huddled together in one large circle behind the one goal rather than in the cramped changing room, Annabel gave them a stern talking to about self-discipline, pride and promotion!

Marshbrook responded. Within thirty seconds of the second half starting, Zara Perry curled an unstoppable shot beyond Gilly – that even if Gilly knew how to save one, she wouldn't have been able to!

Maidens took control. They battered Southsea with shots from long range and short range, shots that hit the post, hit the crossbar, hit Gilly in the face and hit defenders on the hand that the referee somehow didn't spot. They hit everywhere but the back of the net.

Annabel made changes. She swapped players around and she even mumbled, "I wish we still had Leah!" but nothing was working and Southsea held onto their narrow advantage, going into the final minutes of the game.

Annabel looked anxiously at her stopwatch. Sixty seconds left.

"We need a goal!" she bellowed.

"That's obvious!" thought Hannah, though she smiled a cheeky grin and kept her thoughts firmly in her head.

"Even a draw will do!" Annabel crowed.

By now, Leah **was** defending, everyone was. A wall of nine yellow shirted defenders blocked the path between Maidens and Gilly's goal. Only Katy didn't come back to defend, staying up front just in case someone, somehow could kick the ball far enough for her to threaten Maidens goal one last time.

"Shoot! Someone shoot!" roared Annabel.

Daisy flicked the ball a few inches in front of Rita's right foot and she let fly with a powerful shot that span and dipped and poor Gilly didn't know which way to dive.

Lady Luck was wearing a Swallows football kit though and the ball span onto the inside of Gilly's left-hand post, hit Gilly on the back of the head and went behind for a corner.

Gilly looked a little shaky and the referee looked to the touchline and beckoned on Hannah who stood in front of Gilly held up a few fingers to check she wasn't seeing double and stood behind the goal to ensure she was going to be okay.

The referee looked at his watch. Maidens goalkeeper Maddy Baker looked at Annabel to get permission to run up to the other goal and be another player attacking for the vital equalising goal.

Daisy stepped up to take the corner kick with all ten of her teammates waiting to head or volley the ball towards the goal. They knew that Gilly wasn't good enough to save it if the shot was on target. All they had to do was get the ball on target.

Daisy raised one arm – that usually meant a cross to the near post, Gilly's left hand side from where Hannah looked on from behind the netting.

From above, the scene would have looked like a crowded pool table – plenty of red, plenty of yellow and the referee in black among them all. Some players were looking at Daisy as she began her run up, some were looking at one another, eyeball to eyeball and some were jostling for positions.

None of it mattered.

With all the pressure on the importance of the kick, Daisy completely miskicked the ball which dribbled no more than a yard away from the corner flag and behind the goal line.

Rather than retrieve that ball, Hannah kicked one to Gilly that was behind the goal to save them from running too far to get a ball back.

Gilly swung her foot with all her might, sending the ball sailing over the heads of the rapidly retreating Maidens to the lone girl, Katy, stood in acres of space on the half way line.

Katy tried to control the ball but failed to do so, but it didn't matter because it squirmed under her foot into the empty, unguarded half of the field that Marshbrook had previously defended.

The all yellow figure of Katy ran towards the ball as it arced into the vast open spaces. A sea of red Maidens chased after her like police after a criminal. But, Katy won the race, got to the ball first and kicked it effortlessly along the ground into an unguarded net.

The sea of red collapsed in a heap to the floor. A sea of Southsea yellow ran the full length of the field to jump on top of their delighted goalscorer.

In all the noise and commotion, no-one heard the final whistle from the referee. The unthinkable had happened. Mind had won over matter. Psychology had won over skill. The Swallows were flying!

Chapter 8

If Leah's phone had been busy prior to the battle between her current and former team, it was even busier after it.

lee, u beta than we eva thought, come back to us, tilly

lee, u might have cost us promotion, sum friend u r, thorny

Hi Leah, well played today. Days like today, I realise we would've done better keeping you on our side and playing you more often. Regards, Annabel

u r the best player we ever had, tho it wudnt be hard, haha, luv ya, bonnie x

We won, we won, we won, we won, we won. Dad was right, you are great! Hannah X

Mixed emotions were raging through Leah's head. She sat on her bed with a piece of A4 paper divided equally into two. At the top it said 'To re-join or not re-join?' On one side of the line it said, PROS, on the other CONS.

As thoughts entered her head, she jotted them down.

CON: Am the best player at Southsea (big headed I know)
CON: I play every week and wouldn't at Marshbrook (or might not)
PRO: The standard is better at Marshbrook and I might get better if they get promoted
CON: Thorny hates me because I might have cost them promotion.
PRO: I do have some good friends there
CON: I have some good friends at SS
CON: The Wagstaffs are ace!
PRO: erm…

After the erm… she wrote 'I DON'T KNOW WHAT TO DO!' in huge capital letters with a crying face and plenty of underlining under the word DON'T.

When she had calmed down, she ran downstairs to see which of her parents were the least busy.

Dad was trying to show Mikey how to use the controller on the game system and Mum was doing one of those prize-winning crosswords in a woman's magazine.

She decided Mum was the best option.

"Mum," she asked, cautiously. "What if?"

"Told you!" said Jeff, knowingly.

"Told you what, Mum?"

"Your Dad reckons you want to re-join Marshbrook."

"No, well, er, no. Well, er, not want, but…"

"You are thinking about it?"

Leah passed the piece of paper to her Mum.

"CONS 5 PROS 2," she said. "Looks like you are staying at Swallows then?"

"Er… would seem it…" Leah replied, hesitantly.

"But…"

"No but… well, er… maybe…"

"Jeff, pass us that £1 coin that's on the mantelpiece will you, love?" Rose asked.

Leah looked quizzically at her Mum.

"How will that help?" Leah asked.

"You'll see."

Leah shuffled on the sofa and looked intently at her mum.

"Okay, which do you want heads to be? Heads you stay at Swallows, tails you go back to Marshbrook?"

"What about Swallows being tails as they have them?" she giggled nervously.

"Swallows have heads too, champ!" Jeff said.

"Jeff, this is important!"

"Dad, this is important!" the two said almost simultaneously.

"Okay, we'll do it as you said Mum, Heads – Swallows, Tails – Maidens."

Mikey paused the game (he had learnt how to do that) and the four pairs of eyes watched the shiny gold coin spin in the air, landing on the carpet.

"The Queen!" said Mikey.

"Oh," said Leah, "I want-"

"Wanted tails?" Rose asked.

"Er…"

"It's okay, pet, it's what I worked out myself when I was about your age. My Mum asked me if I wanted, oh I can't remember, whether to go out with her shopping or go to the football with my Dad or something. I tossed the coin, heads Mum, tails Dad and the minute it landed tails, my gut reaction said 'Oh, I wanted the other one.' It's one way you can make your mind up."

"But my list said..."

"Yeah, your list came from your head, your gut reaction comes from the heart. Your heart said 'I want to go back' did it not?"

"Yeah, I guess..."

Mikey chirped up. "Is Leah going to be a dragon again?"

"No!" said the three voices.

"Oh," said Mikey. "I liked the dragons. Can I join the Dragons?"

Rose gave Leah a hug.

"Do you want your dad to email the league again, asking you to transfer back to Marshbrook?"

Leah didn't know what to say.

"The coin said..." her Mum said, trying to help.

"My list said..." Leah replied quietly and almost tearfully.

"Sleep on it then," Jeff joined in. "The decision doesn't have to be made today."

"Mum?" Leah enquired, glancing in Rose's direction.

"Yes?"

"I'm really unsure. I'm happy at Southsea but I proved to Marshbrook now that I **could** do it with them and... er... I dunno..."

"Join the dragons!" Mikey shouted, gleefully and unhelpfully.

"MIKEY!" rang out the familiar cry.

"Have you spoken with Luke about it?" Rose asked.

"Not really."

"Why not?"

"He'd have me even more confused than I am already! He would drive me on to be successful but would also want me to be loyal to Hannah and Harry."

"Okay then. Have you spoken to Harry about it?"

"Nope," Leah whispered.

"Perhaps you should."

Leah tapped out a quick message to Harry on her phone and was shocked at the almost instant response saying that he wasn't doing much and that he could meet up with her for a quick chat.

Harry's house was only a couple of streets away and was a brisk walk over the railway bridge but Leah knew not to go there alone and waited for her Dad to drive her round in the car.

"'ello Boy Wonder... Mr 'elmshore!" he said, smiling. "Sit yourselves down and let's 'ave a natter."

Even in the few minutes since the texts, Harry's wife had got the kettle on and arranged a plate full of fancy cakes and biscuits to welcome the Helmshores into their home.

Although Harry had been in football a long time, you would never know looking around his living room. It had very old-fashioned décor, clearly dominated by what Mrs Wagstaff expected a house to look like and there wasn't a single photo of Harry at a football match, nor a football trophy, nor even any photos of daughter Hannah with the Swallows.

"What's up Boy Wonder?" Harry asked.

"The ceiling!" Leah joked nervously.

Harry chuckled before saying, "Come on..."

Leah explained everything slowly and calmly to ensure she didn't cry. Harry listened attentively, resisting the urge to interrupt, while Jeff just sat there munching on a deep-filled individual apple pie or two as cakes and biscuits were something they rarely had in the Helmshore household.

"So, what do I do?" Leah ended her speech with.

Harry looked at her and cleared his throat before speaking.

"You only get one life, one chance, one opportunity. If you go, you go with our blessing. If you stay, we will still let you go if you change your mind. I 'ope that 'elps!"

Chapter 9

Leah was confused.

Probably more confused now than before she went to see Harry.

She knew what her list said; she knew what the tossed coin said. It didn't make it any easier to actually make a decision.

Mum was convinced by the coin method as it showed Leah's gut reaction.

Jeff didn't mind either way – he was just the chauffeur.

Mikey didn't care either. He got upset that Deadtail Dragons didn't have an under 8 team for him to play in, so his Mum decided to enrol him with Beavers instead to give her 'little man' his own hobby.

But, Luke was fuming when Leah told him that the coin method suggested a return to Marshbrook!

Although he was keen on progressing to a higher level of football himself, Luke had vowed never to lose sight of his roots with Deadtail Dragons – however humble those beginnings were.

I can't believe u wanna join Maidens again! kitten x

> *it's the best chance i'll get to progress up the leagues x*

r friends not more important than success? kitten x

> *I have friends at maidens too x*

u shudnt have left in the first place then, kitten x

> *u said u thought I was doing right thing to get games x*

There is no I in 'team', but there is an I in 'selfish'. Luke

Just as Thorny's texts had ended with no friendly kiss, it hadn't gone unnoticed that Luke had signed without a kiss and with his real name rather than his nickname.

Leah's head was a whirlwind, her stomach like a washing machine, spinning fast, spinning slow, sometimes calm and relatively quiet, sometimes extremely loud.

She kept tossing coins, and, like her Mum said, however the coin landed, she either cheered 'yes!' or called out 'best of three,' 'best of five' until she got the result she wanted – to return to Marshbrook.

Despite Luke's texts, she knew what she wanted and told Hannah and Harry that she wanted to move back. Both were gracious and encouraged her to follow her heart. Harry even said, 'you are doing the right thing Boy Wonder!'

If making the decision wasn't hard enough, when Jeff emailed the league to announce their transfer to Marshbrook, they emailed back to state that there was a ruling prohibiting players transferring to another club within the same season. Leah would have to wait four weeks for the transfer to be completed.

The league said she was allowed to still play for Southsea during that period, but Leah thought it fairest that once she had made her decision she should stop playing for the Swallows until the transfer had gone through.

So, after signing off with a win – and a goal – against Holy Cross, she had a couple of weeks off from playing before she could join up with the Maidens again, just in time for the last match of the season.

After the game, her fellow Swallows were all high-fives and hugs wishing her all the best back with Marshbrook.

Ironically, her first game back with Marshbrook was the rearranged fixture with Weston Warriors. She already knew about this ground of course, but until she arrived with her Dad she hadn't realised just how much in the middle of nowhere it actually was!

This time it was a glorious sunny afternoon without a hint of a cloud in the sky and no chance of any rain causing any issues this time!

Leah travelled to the match with Tilly and her Dad as her Mum and Dad both thought it best they picked up Mikey together from his first ever adventure, a sleepover with the Beavers.

Even with a satnav and looking at an online map before they left, Mr Adams drove past the entrance to the correct lane on more than one occasion and just about got the girls to the rest of the team in time for their pre-match chat.

The Warriors were top of the league having won every game they had played and Marshbrook needed a draw to guarantee promotion after Robin's Wood had a surprise defeat the previous week to Daleside Diamonds.

Annabel had decided that Anna Lucas would be included in the team as an extra defender, not that Leah had ever expected to go straight back in the team after her time away.

Anna was a quietly spoken girl who rarely said anything when she did speak. She was the sort of girl who just wanted to be a part of the team. It didn't matter to her whether she played or not, nor whether she came on as sub. She would come along every week and try her hardest regardless.

Leah was still a little disheartened though as she sat on a blue chair at pitch side, but she had learned that at least now Annabel would be prepared to give her a chance if needed.

Despite that, Leah still tapped her heels together or swung her legs in frustration and boredom.

Occasionally, because Luke had always encouraged her to do so, she got up from her seat, stretched her muscles and went for a sprint up and down the touchline to remind Annabel that she was still there and hoped that she might consider giving her a game.

Somehow, Marshbrook were clinging onto a 0-0 score and the Warriors were getting more and more frustrated that everything they tried to do was falling short of getting a goal.

Anna had played the best game of her life, justifying Annabel's selection decision, but having never played so intensely before it was only a matter of time before she couldn't go on and Annabel called Leah over and alerted the referee for a substitution.

Anna could barely high five Leah as they swapped places on the side-line. She was a physical wreck, akin to a runner who has just completed the London Marathon on the warmest day of the year! Sweat was pouring off her hair and face which was as red as her Marshbrook shirt.

Leah sprinted up towards the halfway line to her normal position of striker but Annabel quickly shouted onto the field, "No, Leah, take Anna's place in defence! We only need a draw!"

Leah couldn't defend. Although she watched a lot of football with her Dad and with Luke, and her positional play was actually quite good, her tackling wasn't very good. She continually missed the ball, kicked the opponents' leg and conceded free-kick after free-kick.

After the fourth foul, the referee wagged her finger at Leah and loudly shouted, "No more of those please, number 12!"

Maddy stood on her goal-line, visibly frustrated with Leah. She rolled her eyes and shook her head repeatedly that the Warriors were being given more chances than they had mustered at any stage earlier in the game.

Maddy barked out instructions to position the wall of four girls in front of her to protect the goal.

Leah looked over towards Annabel. She was pointing to her watch and held aloft one finger. They hoped this was the last time they would have to hold out for the draw.

"One minute left," she thought. "Defend this and we have almost certainly got a draw!"

Tilly Adams tugged on Leah's shirt to get her to pull in tighter into the wall. Leah's concentration was usually spot on, but there was something about this chance of getting a draw with clearly the best team in the league that was taking Leah's mind off the game.

The Warriors number seven paced backwards away from the ball, further than she normally would, suggesting she had decided to go for power.

Leah was still glancing in Annabel's direction and trying to count one minute in her head.

"60... 59... 58..." as the Weston player back-paced. "57... 56..." as she sprinted towards the ball.

"55... 54..." as she kicked the ball with all the power she could muster.

"53..."

Leah never got to 52.

Unlike the three other girls in the defensive wall, Leah had taken her eyes off the ball as the kick was taken. We will never know whether Leah would have had time to duck out of the way or felt brave enough to head the ball away if she had been concentrating, but the ball smacked Leah's turned head above the right ear and she collapsed to the ground with a massive thud.

If Leah had been able to carry on counting that minute instead of being out for the count she wouldn't have got to 49 before Annabel sprinted onto the field as fast as she could.

For those looking on, it seemed an age before there was any motion from Leah's body. The sparse crowd were muttering and wondering whether she was conscious or unconscious, whether there was any blood and some of the Warriors fans were unconcerned how long she had been down and just wanted to get on with the game!

Eventually, dazed, Leah was coming round, under continuous examination from Annabel who encouraged her to sit up straight. She could groggily count that Annabel was holding up three fingers and she was helped to her feet and walked off the field using her manager as a crutch!

The referee indicated a dropped ball to the captains of both sides, much to the Warriors disgust as they felt an advantage had been taken away from them.

The ball dropped to the floor, bounced up and Tilly Adams reacted quickest, swinging a leg at it to clear the ball as far as she could.

The full-time whistle blew (again, to the Warriors disgust as they didn't feel it had been anywhere near the minute they believed was left in the game) and the Maidens sprinted as fast as they could to Leah to congratulate her on the point-gaining block!

Leah sat there, not quite sure what they were celebrating and drank water from a sports bottle while one of Annabel's friends held a cold compress on Leah's head.

Leah could make out the figure of Annabel on the phone and a blurred group of Weston players gesticulating angrily towards the referee, but she might as well have been asleep and dreaming it for all she could remember.

After some time, the Warriors ground was a silent arena again with both sets of players back in the changing rooms. Leah's teammates were quickly showered and changed to celebrate their promotion but Leah remained in her football kit.

Maddy and Tilly were quickly arranging a trip to KFC to celebrate and gestured to Leah, 'join us later Hero!"

Chapter 10

"I'm a hero?" Leah questioned, sitting on the benches outside the changing room for some fresh air from the steamy environment of a dozen girls who had just showered!

"An injured one," Annabel stated. "I've tried ringing your parents Leah but there's no answer. Is there anyone else I can ring?"

"My aunt," Leah said. "My phone's in my bag."

Leah swiped her finger to unlock the phone and opened up her contacts list.

"No answer there eith-" Annabel began saying as Miriam's phone went straight to voicemail.

Annabel didn't have time to leave a message as a bustling woman came hurtling over to the side of the pitch.

"Where is she? Where's my niece? What happened to my poppet?"

"How the-?" asked Annabel.

"Get here?" asked Miriam.

"Yeah," said Leah and Annabel together.

"I watch all your matches on that twittery-thingy-ma-bob," Miriam stated.

"You do?" quizzed Leah.

"Yeah, yeah, life in the old dog yet you know? I didn't want one of those trendy phone thingies but the man in the shop said it'd bring me into the 20th Century."

No-one felt it right to tell Miriam that we were in the 21st Century already.

"Now then," said Miriam, pulling a little torch out of her supermarket carrier bag. "Has anyone looked in her eyes yet?"

Leah didn't appear to flinch at the torch shining at her which immediately caused Miriam to say, "Good, good" in an extremely high-pitched voice.

"Can't be too careful with head injuries," Miriam insisted.

"Aunty, I'm okay! A little shaken, but I'll live!"

"You're okay?" Miriam questioned. "There is blood on your shirt."

She was right.

On the back of Leah's shirt were drops of blood; nothing serious, not enough for Leah to even have noticed.

Miriam looked towards Annabel, "I assume the team has a First Aid kit?"

One of the girls scurried across to the bench where the spare footballs and bottles of energy drinks were and handed it to Miriam.

Miriam put on a pair of blue nitrile gloves and rummaged around the kit for a gauze bandage.

She cut off a strip, folded it over a couple of times to increase its thickness and asked Leah to hold it on her head to apply pressure to the wound.

The rest of the team were looking on as Miriam began wrapping the bandage around Leah's head where she was holding with her fingers, eventually removing Leah's fingers out of the way and fastening the bandage with some tape.

One of the girls chuckled that Leah looked like Humpty Dumpty and it raised a smile on Leah's face too.

"Leah, put your fingers back on for a bit of extra pressure, please and we'll get you checked out at the hospital."

"I'll come if you need me to," Annabel stated.

"We'll be fine, thank you, but we've got your number on Leah's phone I assume?"

"Yes, and you should have mine as a failed call on yours anyway, let me know how she gets on," Annabel continued.

"Of course, of course."

Leah left with Miriam, to a rapturous round of applause and cheering from her teammates at their promotion and Leah's heroics.

Thankfully for Miriam, the hospital was only a ten-minute drive away and luckily, once they had reported in to reception, they were queue-jumped to be checked over due to the nature of Leah's potential injury.

"You've done this before, I assume?" the doctor said, looking towards Miriam.

"One or two in my dim and distant past," Miriam replied, almost blushing at the young doctor's compliment.

"Let's take a look," he continued, unwinding the bandage from around Leah's head.

He pushed back the hair from over the wound a few centimetres above Leah's ear and started to clean the wound properly.

"We'll get that stitched up but we'll have to cut away some of the hair to get good access to the wound. It'll grow back," he said.

Leah and Miriam both chuckled.

"What have I said?" asked the doctor.

"It's a long story," said Miriam. "But, let's put it this way, Leah knows one or two things about haircuts."

Leah sniggered again.

"Okay," the doctor said. "Won't take long to sort you out anyway, and," he said, looking at the notes on a clipboard, "as Leah didn't lose consciousness and is clearly in good spirits, as soon as we're done, you will be okay to go home."

Five butterfly stitches later, the two were back in the car and Leah texted Annabel (it was quicker than Miriam doing it) with an update.

"When we get you home, we'll run you a bath, get yourself cleaned up and get into your onesie and lie up watching some TV."

"I said I'd go down the park with Luke though!" Leah complained.

"You're going nowhere until you've cleaned up and we can monitor you for a bit. I still can't get hold of your Mum but I'll stay there until they are back."

"Aunty, I'm okay! I promise!"

Miriam's maternal instincts were kicking in as the car pulled onto the driveway, even to the extent of undoing Leah's seatbelt and taking her hand as she got out of the car, not letting go until they were in the house.

Nor would Miriam let Leah take a bath alone. The doctor had told them the stitches had to be kept dry until they were removed ("up to a week," they were told) so Miriam was making sure Leah remembered that. She was also concerned that the heat of the water and the steam may cause Leah to pass out.

The red mark was still visible from where the ball had struck, close enough to her right eye for a mixture of blues, blacks and purples to appear below her eye.

Miriam led her by the hand to her bedroom and again as they went downstairs, where Leah lay on the sofa watching classic 'Tom and Jerry' cartoons and Miriam came into the room holding a cereal bowl, though Leah couldn't work out from her angle what was in it.

"Move those feet!" she said, tapping Leah on the calf. "Here..." she continued, handing her a bowl of mint choc chip ice-cream.

Leah shuffled up her feet so her aunt could sit down and then lay them down across her lap.

"Thanks!"

"You deserve it. You've been my brave little princess. Most girls would've ducked out of the way, no doubt!"

"I... erm... didn't exactly head it on purpose! The ball kinda hit me more than I hit it!"

"Yeah, so your manager was saying! I was trying to encourage you!"

Leah took a spoonful of ice-cream and sucked it off the spoon.

"I probably gave you too many scoops," Miriam confessed, "so best not tell your mother. Our secret, yeah?"

Leah winked with her left eye (she may have struggled if she had tried to do it with her right black eyed eye)

Eventually, when the spoon could get no more ice-cream, she swished her finger around the bottom of the bowl and slurped down the last remaining bit of ice cream.

"Would you like a drink Leah?"

"Aunty, I **can** do things for myself!"

"I know you can, but I insist you rest up all afternoon!"

Leah smiled.

"I'm surprised Mum and Dad haven't—"

Leah didn't get chance to finish the sentence "haven't text yet" as Miriam's phone beeped and Rose had sent a message, "How is she? Has she kept any food down? Won't be long. Mikey's getting tired. Hopefully will ring you before we're home."

Miriam read the message out to Leah.

"I'll reply," she said. "I'm okay LOL."

She passed the phone and Leah took it in her right palm with her thumb over the display ready to type.

"Aunty..." she said, nervously.

"Yeah?"

"I can't see the words properly."

"What do you mean?"

"They're a bit blurry."

"Can you see the TV okay?"

"Yeah, that's fine. Just this."

"Pass me my phone back, please Leah."

"You ringing Mum?"

Miriam looked through her phone contacts and Leah could hear the faint ringing tone as the phone was pressed against her ear.

No-one was answering at first, but then Leah heard a faint woman's voice answer the phone but still her aunt didn't speak.

She pulled the phone away from her ear and pressed one on the keypad.

She was confused and could hear the ringing tone again against her aunt's ear.

"Hi, I'm ringing from Jeff and Rose Helmshore's – I'm Rose's sister, 96 Courtney Park. Can you send a doctor round please?"

Leah listened carefully as she explained to the on call doctor what had happened and how she might be over-reacting but didn't want to take any chances. Nor did she want to wait for Leah's parents to come home for their opinion.

She hung up the phone and stood up from one end of the sofa to kneel at the other end to put her arm around Leah's shoulder.

"Doc said fifteen minutes. Chances are your parents will be here before that, but I think we should get this checked."

Leah nodded.

"Are you shaking?" Miriam asked, detecting a slight vibration in her hand.

"A little."

"You cold?"

"A little."

Miriam hurried away upstairs to get a blanket.

She didn't get that far.

"Aunt-!" came a terrified scream from the sofa.

She stopped dead in her tracks on the stairs and raced straight back down to see Leah leaning over the edge of the sofa being sick.

It was too late to get a bucket, too late to worry about the laminate flooring.

She put her hand on Leah's shoulder as it was about all she could do to comfort her and nervously looked to the front door to see whether Jeff and Rose or the doctor arrived first.

It was the doctor.

"Has she been persistently sick?"

"No, this is the only time."

"Persistent headache?"

"No. Obviously, she got hit by the ball but she hasn't said so."

"Balance problems?"

"No."

"Double or blurred vision?"

"A little when she got hit and a while ago when she tried to send a text."

"Look," the doctor began. He rubbed his face with his hands then pushed up his glasses as he spoke. "I wouldn't think it's anything more than mild concussion from the football, but let's not 'think', let's check. I am going to recommend we get this checked out at the hospital. Do you have transport?"

"Yes."

"It would be quicker if you drove there rather than waiting for an ambulance."

Leah comprehended what was going on. Her Dad liked watching boxing and she'd seen enough about it to know that a sore head and a ringing in the ears was about right for being bashed with a boxing glove and that a football probably wasn't much different.

Just as Miriam and Leah were about to leave, Jeff and Mum returned behind a running Mikey who immediately noticed the sick on the floor.

The doctor repeated what he had explained to Miriam and advised that a precautionary examination wouldn't do any harm.

"I'll take her!" Rose insisted. "Mikey, go and play with the toys in your room please while Daddy cleans this up. I'll ring you!"

Chapter 11

Rose was relieved that the journey to the hospital was free from any further sickness.

Leah had complained of "feeling tired" a couple of times during the short drive but Rose had insisted Leah had remained awake, for fear that if she had been concussed sleeping could be dangerous.

Thankfully, there weren't too many people waiting in Accident and Emergency and when Rose gave Leah's details the receptionist had already been aware of her imminent arrival.

Leah was taken through to a cubicle where a male nurse explained what the Doctor had told them and suggested that they might need to take some blood samples later.

Leah sat up and rolled up the sleeve of her onesie ready. She wasn't fazed by any of it. Her Mum and Dad both gave blood regularly and she'd sat and watched them donate at the local Methodist Church.

She lay on the hospital bed so she could be monitored that she wasn't sick again, having had a couple of headache tablets as the doctor advised.

Rose watched vigilantly, having to avoid nodding off herself! Leah did sleep for some of the time with a nurse coming in hourly to check she was awake and conscious.

Thankfully, the doctors permitted Rose to send a text from within the vicinity of the hospital bed and she updated Jeff and Mikey back home. They were building a den in the living room with all the sofa cushions before Mikey was eventually carried up to bed for a story (a little later than Rose would have allowed if she had been there!)

Eventually, the door opened and a doctor entered with a clipboard with several pieces of paper clipped to it. Leah was sleeping, so Rose stood up and walked across to the Doctor.

He spoke quietly.

"We'll need to wake Leah again now. I just want to chat with her and see what we feel about letting her go home."

Rose shook Leah's arm gently and she stirred.

"Hi," said the doctor.

"Hi," said Leah.

"Can I ask you a few questions please? Some of them may seem a little silly."

"Yeah."

"Your name please."

"Leah... Leah Helmshore."

"Good, do you know where you are?"

"Yeah, Mum brought me into hospital."

"Do you know why?"

"Yeah, I was sick in the living room."

"Do you know why that was?"

"I was playing football earlier and the ball hit me on the head."

"What day is it?"

"Sunday."

"Good."

Rose smiled.

The doctor continued, "Leah's been here a good while now. She's not been sick again and has responded to the questions. It's clear she knows what has happened and where she is."

Leah smiled. They were the easiest test questions she had ever had in her life!

"We can't say for certain if there will be any delayed or continued concussion, but we want to monitor her overnight. We'll need to come and see her during the night, wake her up every couple of hours or so, ask her a few questions. Come the morning, we'll decide whether we need to conduct a scan to see if anything shows up."

"Okay, doctor. Thank you."

He patted Rose reassuringly on the arm and left the room. Rose walked over to give Leah a kiss, sat down in the chair next to her bed and put her arm around Leah's shoulder.

Rose had tried to be strong but couldn't control it any longer and the tears started flowing from her eyes.

She put her jacket over her upper body and tried to get some rest, knowing full well she'd spend most of the time looking across at Leah.

Morning came and Jeff called in at the hospital on his way to work, Mikey having had another away from home adventure staying at Aunt Miriam's.

"Hey," he whispered.

Rose woke, although she wasn't fully asleep anyway.

"Is my little champ okay?"

"Seems it yeah, no sickness and she hasn't said she's got a headache. Got a lovely black eye though!"

"You told them at work?"

"Yeah, my boss text back just after you'd said you'd gone to bed last night. I'll ring the school soon enough and let them know that I'll be keeping her home to keep an eye on her. You spoke to Miriam about Mikey?"

Leah woke before Jeff could answer.

"Hey champ! What's it like being promoted?"

"Good Dad, yeah, really good! Must've been some party after the game because I think I have a hangover!"

The doctor came in to assess Leah's health and had a quiet word with Rose before speaking directly to Leah.

"Leah, we've decided that we will do a scan. There's absolutely nothing to worry about, but it's better to be certain. The head is a delicate object and it won't do any harm to see exactly what's happened with that football impact."

Leah nodded and held her Mum's hand.

In truth, Leah's main concern was whether she was going to get any breakfast and eventually a nurse came in to ask her what she wanted to eat and drink.

While Leah was eating, the nurse explained that the doctor would inject a dye into her to make the pictures clearer in the scanner, but that it wouldn't hurt and she didn't have to worry.

Leah didn't look anywhere near worried as her Mum did! The nurse had managed to convince her it was 'an adventure' and that very few children were as special as she was to experience this machine.

The consultant came in and explained in more detail. "The machine we use is called an MRI scanner. It uses magnets to scan the body from top to toe."

Leah nodded.

"It's very important, Leah," he said, "that you keep still else it will ruin the picture – like a photograph. If you think you will be unable to keep still, we can give you an injection, but at your age I think you will be able to lie still for us?"

She nodded again.

"I'm going to be totally honest with you, Leah," he stated. "The scanner is very noisy. You can wear special headphones that will allow you to listen to music and if you want to take a toy in with you, you can, as long as it doesn't contain any metal."

In the importance to get to the hospital quickly, they hadn't given any thought to the fact that Leah might be staying in overnight, but at least having already been in her onesie, she had been set for the night's sleep.

Of course, it did have a very long metal zip, so Leah had to slip into a hospital gown and the nurse checked that Leah wore neither earrings nor rings.

The consultant, nurse and Rose walked alongside Leah as a hospital porter pushed her in a wheelchair down several long corridors.

In the room, Leah met Mr Harris, the Radiographer – a very short man with the darkest, shiniest hair Leah had ever seen, protruding from a cap on his head!

Mr Harris began, "Leah, you can call me Simon. I'm the one that puts you into the machine, but, don't worry, I let you out too!"

Rose didn't find that comment very funny but Leah sniggered as she had worked out it was to make her feel at ease.

"This is the scanner," he continued. "We will put you in this tunnel here, head first."

He then pointed to the window on the other side of the room.

"The other side of that window is the super-duper mega-computer. We can't put it in the same room because—"

"Computers use magnetism to make them work," Leah interrupted confidently.

"Correct!" Simon replied. "But, I will be able to talk to you through an intercom and you can talk back to me. We shouldn't have to talk too much. You just need to stay as still as you can and we will get you out of there much quicker!"

Leah put her thumbs up.

"I will watch you on a TV monitor in there, checking you haven't run away or anything," Simon said, winking.

Leah chuckled again.

"Leah's Mum," Simon said. "Do you want to stay in the waiting room or come in the room with me? It's entirely your choice..."

Rose followed Simon.

"The scan should take about twenty minutes," he said. "Just keep still and listen to what I say please. We've never yet had the scanner swallow anyone up, but there's always a first time," he said again, with a cheeky wink from his left eye.

Leah was helped from her wheelchair onto the scanner bed while Rose looked on. Mr Harris pressed a button on the side of the scanner which raised the bed to a height just above the lip of the tunnel.

He reached for the headphones and handed them to Leah and placed a lemon-shaped object into her left hand connected to a wire. He explained that it was to be squeezed if she wanted to stop, but also pointed out that they would have to start again if she did stop, so to "stick it out if you can."

A separate frame was placed over her head "to take a better picture," Mr Harris stated.

Another set of buttons on the side of scanner, looking very similar to the buttons on an X-box or PlayStation controller, were pressed and Leah moved, like shopping on a supermarket conveyor belt, into the scanner.

She stopped part way with just her head inside the scanner. She had been told she would go into it in stages, to gently ease her into the situation without panicking her.

She could hear Mr Harris press the buttons again and she went further into the scanner, this time as far as her waist before she stopped again. She didn't end up going all the way in, the lowest part of her legs and her bare feet were sticking out the bottom of the machine.

Mr Harris spoke to Leah to check she was alright and left the room to watch through the television monitor in the adjacent room.

Rose didn't want to watch on. She knew she wouldn't understand enough about the images on the screen and was worried that she would see something and worry what it was even if it was perfectly normal to the radiographer looking on.

Leah hadn't got a clue how long she was in the machine for. She had tried to count the number of songs on the CD and work out that each one would be about four minutes long. But, like counting sheep at night-time, counting songs while listening to them was hypnotic and she was pretty sure she fell asleep.

She came out the scanner as slowly as she went in and again she was transferred back into the wheelchair and pushed back onto the hospital ward.

A nurse explained to Leah that the results could take "a very long time" and whispered to Rose that this "could be several days."

Rose was getting impatient sat in the hospital ward while Leah sat up still listening to music. She had asked Jeff to bring Leah some 'going home clothes' in the morning when he had called in, but he had forgotten in the rush. So, they were sat there waiting for his return from picking Mikey up after school and nipping home to get Leah something to change into.

Eventually, the two Helmshore males rushed in, Mikey first, throwing his arms around his sister before realising he might have hurt her by not being careful enough.

Jeff passed a carrier bag of clothes to Leah and he, Rose and Mikey stepped away, pulling the hospital bed's curtain behind them to allow Leah the privacy of getting changed.

Leah pulled back the curtain.

"Not bad!" she exclaimed, wearing blue jeans, a white T shirt, and a burgundy cardigan. "I feared what clothes you would bring me Dad! A girl likes to co-ordinate!"

Jeff laughed.

"Is she good to go?" he asked.

"Oh yes!" Rose said, exasperatingly. "She's been good to go for about two hours! Lack of clothes was what was stopping us going home!"

"Okay, okay!" Jeff responded, apologetically. "Let's go troops!"

Chapter 12

Leah looked at herself in the mirror. Like most girls' bedrooms, the mirror was an important central feature.

She had always been conscious of looking nice, whether smart in her school uniform or in casual clothes in the evenings.

Even with the shortened boyish hair of her Deadtail Dragons days, she had got it done fairly regularly to look neat and tidy.

But, although there were elements of teasing when she had the short hair, she was not as self-conscious then as she was now of the clump of hair that was missing from the right-hand side of her head.

At least, she only had a week of school to get through with the clump. She returned to the local health centre on the following Monday where the stitches were finally removed, with no further bleeding from the wound.

"All done," said the doctor. "All better. Keep an eye on it, and if the wound re-opens let us know as soon as you can."

Leah smiled.

Rose took a close inspection at the healing wound and wondered if there would be a permanent scar.

The doctor could tell Rose wanted to ask something.

"Scars are unpredictable," he stated. "It could clear fully in a few months or be there forever…"

"A permanent reminder of your football heroics!" Jeff said proudly.

"The Harry Potter of football!" Leah chuckled.

As ever, Rose didn't seem too amused that her princess had a 'war wound' as she muttered under her breath.

Jeff shook the doctor's hand, as did Leah, while Rose said a quiet, "Thank you Doctor" before the three of them were back in the car.

"Home, James!" Leah said confidently.

"Nope champ!" said Jeff.

"No?"

"No," Rose interjected. "Somewhere else we need to go first."

Leah looked puzzled.

She couldn't work out what direction Dad was driving the car in either. It certainly wasn't the way home.

Left at the traffic lights and right at the next lights and the car was driving down the High Street past the butchers, past the opticians and Jeff put the left indicator on, to pull into a small car park behind the library and pizza place.

"Pizza for a hero!" Leah shouted.

"Nope," Jeff said, "other side of the road."

"Gino's!" Rose stated. "No daughter of mine is going round with a clump of hair missing!"

"Linzi!" Leah called, dashing into the salon.

"Hey Lee! Or are you Leah again?" Linzi asked, jumping up from her seat, partly in excitement that she had a customer at last after a very dead hour or two where no-one had come in.

"She's Leah again, sort of," Rose said, gently turning Leah's head round to show Linzi the clump of missing hair and stitches scar.

"Oooh, what you done there?"

"Football injury!" Leah said proudly, standing up straight and sticking out her chest making herself look soldier-like.

"Your thoughts, Linzi?" Rose asked. "It's not shaven where they put the stitches but it will need neatening up."

"Yeah, let me see what I can do."

Leah got into the chair and Rose stood very close to Linzi as she was about to get the scissors near to the stitches mark.

Rose took a sharp intake of breath as the scissors got close to the wound and made Linzi jump.

"Please!" Linzi said. "I'm nervous as it is, not to hurt her. I don't need to jump in the air like a Jack in the Box!"

"Please, Mum!"

"Please, Rose!"

Rose sat down next to Jeff and he handed her a weekly puzzle magazine and a pen and told her to take her mind off things.

"Was your Mum this bad at the hospital?" Linzi whispered in Leah's ear.

Leah sniggered. "A little bit."

Linzi snipped away, stood back, gently straightened Leah's head, bent down a little and tried to make sure that Leah's hair was level on both sides, snipped a little bit off the left hand side to level it up.

She called over to Rose. "I can neaten it up further with the shaver if you wish me to. I think I ought to."

Jeff prodded Rose who was engrossed in the crossword.

"Do what needs doing, Linzi please."

Linzi unhooked the electric shaver from a hook beneath the counter and putting the blades against a metal comb, making her hand and Leah's head vibrate too, she whirred away to finish off.

"Ta-da!" she said, returning the shaver to its hook and lifting a mirror from a hook on the opposite side to show Leah the back of her hairstyle.

Jeff smiled at his princess.

Rose did too.

"All grown up," Rose said.

"Better than the shaven hair last time you came," Linzi chuckled.

Rose handed over the money to Linzi and then the three of them crossed to the pizza place to pick up something for the way home, collecting Mikey en route from Miriam's.

Leah asked if she could grab a few slices and take them up to her room because she had a bit of homework she needed to do and could research it online while she was eating.

She got the okay from her Mum and lay on her bed, the laptop in front of her.

She opened up Google.

It wasn't homework she wanted to look up.

'Head injuries' she typed in.

She wished she hadn't.

By the time she had googled head injuries and MRI scans she had convinced herself she either had brain damage or cancer.

She wept.

She rubbed her eyes and looked at the calendar on the wall. She had crossed out each day one at a time at the start of the month but since the Weston game and her scan she had put big question marks waiting for the results to come back from the hospital as to what, if anything, the scan showed.

She texted Luke.

Despite her little disagreement over the transfer back to Marshbrook, they had agreed to disagree and he still supported her at matches whenever he could and she wanted to talk to someone, other than her parents.

Leah, all you can do is wait X

> *I have waited all season for everything! I think I have no patience left! What if it's something bad?*

If it's something bad, they would have kept you in hospital until they got the results. They would have rushed them through. Stop panicking! X

> *Ok. Waiting for the results is worse than the scan was :'(*

Be strong Boy Wonder! You're a winner! Kitten X

Chapter 13

The house phone rang.

No-one rang it very often. Like many households, it was there because people needed one to have an internet connection. Nearly every phone call Jeff and Rose made or received were via their mobiles.

Jeff looked at the number on the display. He knew that withheld and international numbers usually were cold-callers trying to sell them double-glazed windows or were about some insurance claim with their bank. This was a local dialling code though.

He answered.

"Mr Helmshore?" said the voice down the other end of the phone.

"Who's asking?" he replied, just in case it was a cold-caller.

"It's the Doctor's Surgery here. We have the information back from the hospital regarding Leah. We can get you to see a doctor within the next hour if it suits you. We have 11.10, 11.40 and 12.00 if any of those are any good?"

Jeff consulted with Rose.

"We'll come at 12.00. Leah's at school though. Will we need her?"

"No, the doctor has put a little note on to say Leah doesn't need to attend."

They walked down to the surgery and sat apprehensively until a bleep signified the name was about to change on the illuminated screen and 'Miss Leah Helmshore' flashed up.

They walked down to Room 6 of the surgery, knocked the door and the Doctor beckoned them to two empty seats in front of her desk.

"Leah at school?" she asked.

"Yeah... erm... the receptionist said we wouldn't need her here. Do we?"

"No," she stated. "I just wanted to show you the radiographer's images."

The Doctor had a computer monitor on her desk and she turned it round so Jeff and Rose could both see.

The screen saver was still on at the moment but she swished the mouse to free that up and a sideways on picture of a brain scan showed on the screen.

The Doctor went through the basic facts first.

In the top left hand corner it said 'Helmshore, L', Leah's date of birth and an F for female.

The top right corner showed the name of the hospital, the date and time of the scan and the radiographer's name.

Rose looked quizzingly as if to say, "Why is this relevant?"

The Doctor must have read her mind.

"I just wanted to point those out so we can be absolutely certain that we are showing you the right scan for the right child. It's been known in the past that we've had patients of the same name but different dates of birth, so we have to be certain we have this right."

Jeff nodded in understanding.

"Now," she continued. "Quite simply, to put some context on this image, you first went to the doctor because –"

"Leah got struck by a football from close range at pace. She vomited and was struggling at times with her eyes," Jeff interrupted.

"Yes..." the Doctor paused. "Well, the scan shows evidence of a slight swelling where the ball struck her, which is consistent with the bruising around her ear and eye. But, the swelling is minimal and will clear with plenty of rest."

Rose looked relieved and grasped Jeff by the hand, smiling as she did so.

"She'll have to avoid all physical activity for at least three weeks though – no football, no P.E. at school – and if she complains of any headaches during that time, then come back and we will re-scan if necessary."

"It's a good job that was the last game of the season then!" Jeff exclaimed. "It'd kill her having to wait three weeks to play again after the season she's already had!"

"Any questions?" asked the doctor.

Rose burst into tears.

"Mrs Helmshore?" the doctor questioned.

"It's okay," she said, wiping a tissue across her eyes. "I had so many thoughts in my head... so glad that it was nothing serious!"

"Yes, everything will be fine. Just time to heal now."

Leah was surprised to see both her parents at the school gate when the school bell rang and the teacher had given them permission to leave the classroom.

Leah sprinted over.

"Hey champ!" Jeff called.

"Come here!" called Rose.

Rose threw her arms around her daughter to give her an almighty hug. "The results are back, Leah. Just bruising. You'll need three weeks off P.E. though!"

"YES!" shouted Leah, so loudly that several parents and children turned round to see what was going on. "It was cross country for the next few weeks so I'll get to miss that! Result!"

"Haha," chuckled Jeff. "It'll come around before you know it."

"That's something that can wait!"

Leah smiled.

After the initial excitement of the meeting, the Helmshore females stood there silently, looked at each other and before either of them could say anything, they began to cry and threw themselves into another hug.

Jeff joined in the hug with his left arm around Rose and his right around Leah.

"Mum..." sobbed Leah. "I... thought... I had..."

"Shush, shush darling," Rose said, tearfully. "I know. **We** both feared the worst too. The scan... that machine... what the results would show."

"Aww come on you two!" Jeff interrupted. "When I was playing football..."

"DAD!" Leah spoke. "We know! Boots were proper leather, none of these plastic carpet slippers the players wear these days, the balls were leather and got wet and heavier and heading them was like a brick!"

Leah chuckled.

"We've heard these stories a hundred times!"

"A million!" Rose added.

"A cazillion!" Leah stated, using a word Mikey would have used if he had been there with them!

Leah's Head of Year walked over to see what was going on.

"It's okay," Jeff said. "The waiting is over. Her brain's perfectly normal after all!"

Mr Stravinsky smiled, patting Jeff on the back. "Glad it's all sorted. Leah's not been her normal chatty self at school. Will be good to have the real Leah back!"

Chapter 14

Luckily for Leah, the end of season presentation and disco came after the three weeks of no physical activity had passed. It meant she could enjoy dancing with her friends (and Luke) at the party.

It was the thirtieth anniversary of the girls' league being formed so representatives of all the local teams were in attendance, including Harry and Hannah Wagstaff and the Southsea Swallows players.

Leah was quick to bustle over to them to show them where the butterfly stitches had been and the raised brown scab of the healing skin. Harry rubbed his hand on the shortened hair on Leah's head.

"'Ow nice to 'ave my Boy Wonder back again!" he chortled.

Leah gave Hannah a hug.

"No hard feelings, boss?" she asked.

"Of course not!" Hannah replied. "The time you were with the Swallows was very valuable to us and sometimes you just have to make the best choice for you."

"Thanks!" Leah said, smiling. "See you later, I promised Luke a dance."

"Dancing eh?" Harry said. "'Annah, will you do me the 'onours."

"Of course, Dad."

"Ladies and Gentlemen!" bellowed a voice from the stage, as the music came to an end and those few who were dancing, shuffled off back to their respective seats.

Luke wasn't much of a dancer, so Leah spent most of the evening with her teammates whilst Luke sat in the corner bored as anything. In fact, it was just like being a goalkeeper – spending most of the time observing the proceedings and being ready for anything that might happen!

One thing Luke did observe was that every time there was a dance, Mr Wagstaff was always out there.

'For an old 'un,' Luke thought, 'he certainly is putting some energy into the evening.'

Traditionally, each team in the league had their own individual end of season celebration, but as it was a momentous year in the league's history, the men in suits that make all the decisions invited all the teams to attend the one event.

The sheer numbers of those in attendance did mean that at times it was like the January sales, people jostling between one another, elbows barging, feet kicking, either to get a seat or to get to the refreshment bar.

That said, everyone seemed to be having a good time – all except Luke who was still bored – while Harry Wagstaff seemed to be having the most fun of all.

With meticulous timing, the clock struck 9pm and an oldish chap in a dark suit stood on the stage and announced that the presentations were about to begin.

Those who had seats turned them round to face the stage, everyone else formed a ring around the dancefloor to try and create space for the winners to go forward and collect their trophies.

Leah wasn't particularly interested at this stage – she knew she hadn't won anything with her stop-start season, and although Marshbrook had won promotion, Annabel had told them that there would not be individual medals for the Maidens squad.

She tried to remain enthusiastic though as team after team, player after player, went up to collect trophies that varied in height from fifteen to thirty centimetres, usually marble effect at the bottom with a small gold plaque on, with a gold footballer on top.

She noted that most of the trophies presented had either a male footballer or a football on the top of it. She wasn't sure if football trophies with girl figures on actually existed, but she made a mental note to google it when she got home.

It was gone 10pm by the time the official business of the evening had been done and the dancefloor was about to re-open for the final hour or so of the evening.

Just as the old man with the microphone was about to finish up for the night, with his duties all done, Annabel bustled forward onto the stage and whispered in the man's ear.

"Ladies and gentlemen," he said one last time, "Miss Annabel Davies would just like to say a few words if you could just bear with us a few more seconds before you strut your stuff again on the dancefloor."

Leah was among many girls who cringed at the use of the expression 'strut your stuff' but she eagerly looked towards the stage as Annabel had the microphone in her left hand, ready to speak.

It wasn't obvious at first, but as soon as she began to talk, you could see that the microphone was shaking in her hands, somewhat nervously.

"Good evening, I shan't keep you," she began.

There were more than a couple of quiet voices that whispered, "Good!"

"After a long time in the game, more years than I care to remember," she continued, "I have reached the conclusion that the season that has just finished will be my last."

Leah and the rest of the Maidens gasped!

"I have spoken with the league to resign as manager of Marshbrook Maids with immediate effect and our website, just about now," she said, looking at her watch, "will have an advert on asking for applications for a new manager. I want to thank everyone here, teammates and opponents for a very enjoyable – ahem – number of years in the game. Thank you."

Annabel stepped aside, trying hard not to let her face crack with a frown or a tear and handed the microphone back to the old man who no-one knew the name of!

"Ladies and gentlemen," he uttered, "Miss Annabel Davies."

He motioned Annabel back to stand alongside him.

"Just before you go, Annabel, if I may call you that," he said, holding her by her lower arm as if to stop her escaping. "In recognition of all that you have done for the local game over the last, I best not say, years, we have been in touch with the Football Association and they have presented us with some tickets for the upcoming England Women fixture against France on June 6th."

Annabel looked stunned.

She looked in the envelope and looked even more stunned. She flicked through the tickets to see how many there were but got interrupted by the man whispering, "Twenty, enough for you and your whole team."

Annabel snatched back the microphone and, bursting with excitement, shouted, "There are twenty tickets Maidens! We're off to watch the Lionesses!"

There were a few mumbled comments of, "Not fair!" from some of the players of other teams if you listened carefully enough, but they were drowned out by the "Wahoo", "Get in!", "Nice one!" and general hullabaloo and cheers from the Maidens players.

Then, in a moment that brought much amusement, Annabel grabbed back the microphone, hollered through it, "The dancefloor is re-opened!" and jumped off the stage and waited for someone to join her for a dance! Harry Wagstaff, for a change, looked decidedly unkeen to dance but Hannah gave him a gentle push in the back to direct him towards Annabel!

Leah dragged Luke back onto the floor, almost kicking and screaming but once he had relaxed a bit, Luke appeared to be a rather accomplished dancer.

"'e's been watching 'Strictly Come Dancing'!" Harry chuckled as he and Hannah glided past Leah and Luke on the dancefloor.

Leah laughed.

Luke hadn't heard what Harry said. He was full of concentration in his dance moves!

It was hard to put a finish time on an event that was attended by teams from age 11 up to age 18 but the younger teams **had** tended to drift away at sensible times for their age group. Leah and Luke were two of the youngest still there by the time the proceedings were wound up at just after 11pm.

Jeff picked them up and dropped Luke home, Leah holding tightly onto the ticket for the England match that Annabel had passed to them before the girls dispersed.

Leah couldn't contain her delight as she bounded up the stairs to show her Mum – a delight that was curtailed when her Mum glared at her when Mikey had been woken up!

"Sorry Mum!" she apologised, creeping into her bedroom, flicking over a page of her calendar and writing on it "England match" scribbling a few circles around it, not to mention a huge smiley face.

Chapter 15

June 6th couldn't come quickly enough. Leah wasn't too good at her seven times table to know exactly how many days it had been since the presentation evening, but every single day had been crossed off the calendar on her wall with a thick red pen.

It didn't help that June had been on the next page as she painfully crossed off every day in May! Finally though, she had flipped over the page to June a few days ago and it was finally the morning of the big game!

It was only a friendly match for the Lionesses but that didn't matter to the Maidens as they met outside the Marshbrook ground where Annabel had organised a 17-seater minibus as a few of the players were going there directly in their Dad's car.

It didn't take long for "I Spy" to get boring, complicated by the fact that on a motorway things that are spied soon disappear from view!

Leah introduced her fellow Maidens to a game she was taught by her grandfather – 'First one to spot'. This started with easy ones like 'First one to spot an Eddie Stobart lorry' and got more challenging with ones like 'First one to spot a woman driving a yellow car!'

The journey to the match was trouble free and they congregated in the car park until the children that had come in cars were texted to say where the minibus had parked.

It hadn't been planned that way, but eighteen of the Maidens girls had a white England football shirt on – Leah didn't own the white one, she only ever liked the red away shirt and amongst her teammates she stuck out like a poppy in a field of white petal daffodils!

The children were quite shocked at how organised the Football Association had been with the tickets! They hadn't noticed the numbers on the tickets previously but they were pleasantly surprised to find they were on three different rows, six on the front row, right by the half way line, seven on the row behind and the final seven on the row behind them.

"Ooh, much better than twenty of us on the same row where we can't talk to each other!" Annabel said, with a surprised twee intonation to her voice.

Annabel had handed out the tickets randomly to whoever's hand was nearest to her at the time and they took their seats, sitting down for now at least, with Leah on the front row between Daisy Ferguson and Maddy Baker, who was beaming from ear to ear as this was her "best birthday ever!"

The girls weren't sat down for long.

The pre-match warm up was taking place and the girls were very excitable and were jumping up and down, waving to the players, screaming for someone to sign their matchday programmes and, generally, just hoping to get noticed.

For all of their commotion though, the England Women remained fully focused on their warm up routine so the girls gave up making noise and began taking photos of the players and selfies – of course – of their big day out.

The England Women were greeted by rapturous applause as they entered the field of play and everyone stood proudly as both 'God Save the Queen' and 'La Marseillaise' boomed over the Public Address system.

The Lionesses white kit shone in the afternoon sunshine and within a mere thirty seconds of the game kicking off, the crowd had erupted when England took the lead with a rasping shot from thirty yards out from Toni Duggan which left the French keeper grasping at thin air.

The Maidens were in party spirit as England made it 2-0 with a typical long range strike from England defender Lucy Bronze.

The 45 minutes flew by and the girls were loving every kick of the game – the pinnacle of the women's sport and what they all hoped to achieve in their own careers.

The English and French players retreated to the halfway line and down the tunnel after the referee's whistle brought the first half to its conclusion, and for a split second at least there was a simmering hush around the stadium.

That didn't last long though as thousands of supporters flocked to the refreshment bars and toilets, and colourful and white seats re-emerged to reveal the letters that spelt out the name of the home ground.

Out onto the field came a group of people in tracksuits – a man holding a portable microphone and two women holding luminous bright yellow footballs.

"At half-time today," he began, "we have a keepy-uppy challenge!"

The two women players began to juggle the balls they had from head to foot, to knee, to shoulder to demonstrate what a keepy-uppy was if there was anyone in the crowd that needed to know!

The man continued. "We will run round shortly and select half a dozen young fans to participate in this challenge, so make some noise and we'll see if you are selected!"

Although there were plenty of empty seats during the interval, there were still plenty of children in the ground and still plenty of noise!

None of the Maidens had gone to get refreshments as they had smuggled in sweets and soft drinks in their bags. So, the twenty of them (Annabel included) were waving their arms, jumping up and down and making a commotion in the hope to get noticed.

And they were.

One of the two ladies spotted the red shirt of Leah amongst the white and came over to speak to her!

"Hi, your name is?"

"Leah," she responded.

"Do you play for a team? Do you fancy taking the challenge?"

"Yeah, yeah she does!" said one of her teammates. "We are Marshbrook Maids."

"Fancy it then?" the lady asked.

"Go on Lee!" Maddy said excitedly.

"Er, yeah, but…"

"But what?" the lady asked.

"It's Maddy's birthday today," Leah said, pointing to her teammate stood next to her. "If anyone should, she should!"

"Okay, Maddy it is then!" said the lady, who they later found out was a former England player who had retired a few summers ago.

"Whoa! Wait a minute, you div!" Maddy said to Leah. "I am a goalkeeper, I can't do a keepy-uppy to save my life!"

The others laughed. They knew Maddy was right.

"Besides," Maddy continued, "it was you that was picked and you are the keepy-uppy queen of Marshbrook!"

Leah rubbed her hand over her hair where she'd had it cut a bit shorter by Linzi. She wasn't sure she really wanted to be seen in public like this (even though she looked fine, she was understandably a bit self-conscious since the stitches)

Something in her head was telling her that she would never get a second chance to make a first impression in front of so many people.

Before she even had time to say, "Okay, I'll do it," her legs had taken the lead and she had clambered over the advertising hoardings onto the perimeter of the pitch and was led onto the field by the former England International.

She ran off to get another contestant while the other lady and the man also came back with two youngsters, the ages ranging from 10 to 14, three boys and three girls.

The first lad, Rhys from Cardiff, claimed to be a distant relative of Wales player Gareth Bale but there were a few looks of disbelief from the rest of the Maids.

He had skills though and as the crowd slowly filtered back to their seats with hot dogs, drinks and crisps galore, Rhys managed 83 keepy-uppies before he lost his balance and the ball thudded into the green turf.

Lauren, an 11-year-old from Shropshire, was next up and started well, getting to sixty in rapid time but her brisk start burned her out quickly and she struggled to 77 and collapsed in a heap on the grass.

Next up was a 13-year old scouser by the name of Damon and he effortlessly passed Rhys' 83, got a huge round of applause from the crowd when he got to 100 and every kick after that was cheered with great gusto! Eventually, his 100 became 150 and Leah looked on knowing that anything near 200 would probably be too much for her to beat.

The crowd whooped with delight as Damon reached 200 before he got over-confident, tried to show off, lost control of the ball almost straightaway, ending on 202.

Teenager Bethany was an anti-climax after Damon's skills and managed only 46 while the youngest contender, 10-year old Paul had clearly never done them before and managed eight the first time and was given another go and got to 23 which he seemed delighted with!

Which left Leah.

She was handed one of the balls and already felt confident as it was the same one Damon had used several minutes earlier.

The man with the microphone asked her a few questions about her and when Leah mentioned the name of the side she played for her Maidens teammates let out a huge cheer from beside the touchline.

Luckily for Leah, the hot June sun disappeared behind a cloud for a while and she gently juggled the ball between her two feet to limber up a little bit, slowly counting to twenty in her head. Slowly but surely her confidence grew and her skills became more elaborate, using her head (carefully aware of her stitches' scar) and shoulders.

In time, Leah forgot the crowd were there and kept control of the ball as if she was in her own back garden with only brother Mikey watching on. She vaguely heard the crowd cheer when she thought she was on 100 but she had even lost count herself as her concentration was purely on keeping the ball off the ground.

She knew she was doing well. Her muscles were beginning to ache, so she knew she had to be somewhere near her best score.

Someone in the crowd shouted, "She's gonna do it!" awakening Leah's awareness of being inside a football stadium and not on her back lawn.

A huge cheer went up as Leah reached 200 (already past her personal best)… 201… 202… 203… she had done it! She had won!

Some sort of adrenalin rush hit Leah as the cheers rang around the ground and instead of continuing, she had a sudden urge to shoot for goal!

Despite being in the centre circle of the pitch, the ball span off Leah's head onto her right foot and she launched it towards the goal to the right of where her friends and manager were sitting.

The crowd were aghast!

Tens of thousands of eyes were focused on the ball that left Leah's foot and rapidly travelled towards the goal. The ball slowly descended onto the turf about twenty metres from the open goal and it seemed every man, woman and child watched the spherical object as it bounced on the ground almost perfectly central to the white frame of the goal.

Another bounce took the ball towards the penalty spot and it continued slowly towards its target.

A couple of bounces later and the ball's momentum had truly slowed and Leah's world was in slow motion to see if she had managed to score a goal from the halfway line!

It was trickling now and the crowd were gasping as the ball stopped less than a centimetre away from crossing the line!

"Unbelievable!" cried the man on the microphone alongside Leah in the middle of the pitch. "But, ladies and gentleman, boys and girls, with 203 keepy-ups, we have our winner... give it up for Leah Helmshore!"

The second half of the match was a blur to Leah. She was dreaming big! Keepy-ups at Wembley Stadium, not as a spectator though, as an England international! Not to mention the Captain's armband on her shirt sleeve.

But, back in the real world, England's Toni Duggan made it 3-0 and the Lionesses held on to a nervous finish when France pulled two goals back in two minutes just before the end.

The final whistle blew and the home supporters cheered loudly as they made their ways home. Leah was still beaming from ear to ear from her half-time display as she got into the minibus.

"You are lucky you can get in," Maddy joked. "Am sure that head's very big right now!"

Leah punched Maddy in a jovial manner on her right shoulder.

Leah bounded through the front door and told her parents all about the half-time interval, even though she had already sent them several texts throughout the second half telling them all they needed to know!

"Proud of you champ!" Jeff said, giving his daughter a hug.

"It's been a weird season hasn't it, Dad?" she asked.

"Yup!" he agreed.

"And that's it, all over now until pre-season training in late July. Another thing to wait for!"

"Enjoy the summer! Forget about football for a couple of months and start again afresh!"

Forgetting about football wasn't easy when Leah's bedroom was covered from ceiling to floorboard in football posters and other football related memorabilia.

But, forget it she had to. She had a month or so of school to get through and then pre-season would begin the Thursday before they broke up for the summer holidays.

Her calendar for July only had two comments – "Pre-Season training UGH" with a sad face and the following day "summer holidays" with a huge smiley face.

That was until she came home from school to see her Mum stood there holding an envelope.

"For me?" Leah asked.

"Yup!"

Rose handed it to Leah.

She checked that it was addressed to her and noted the Football Association logo in the top left hand corner of the envelope neatly level with the first class stamp.

"Open it! Open it!" Mikey screamed excitedly.

Leah nervously lifted up a corner of the seal of the envelope, made a small hole and carefully slid her finger along to open it.

She pulled out the letter which also had the Association logo on the header of the paper.

To the parents/guardians of Leah Helmshore (Marshbrook Maids)

We are writing, firstly, to congratulate Leah on her performance at the England versus France match in the half-time keepy-up challenge.

You may be aware that there were several such challenges at other England Men and England Women internationals throughout the season.

In total, there were twelve half-time winners, including Leah. We would like to invite her to Wembley Stadium on November 29th to compete against the other eleven children at another keepy-up challenge.

Would you please complete and sign the permission slip below and return it to the F.A. Headquarters to state whether you can attend.

Please also state how many tickets you would like for the match (include Leah in this total). We will provide a maximum of four complimentary tickets but you can also order additional ones if required.

We look forward to hearing from you.

There was then an illegible signature above the words "Chief Executive of the Football Association" in blue ink.

Leah ran upstairs as quickly as she could.

"Where are you going?" Rose asked.

"To check something!" Leah called back.

Leah returned to where her Mum and Mikey were standing.

"What were you checking?" she asked. "Surely you haven't got much planned for November already have you?"

"No, I haven't! But that's not what I was checking!"

"Oh?"

"I was checking we were not in April! Surely this is an April Fool's joke!"

"It looks official enough to me, Leah!" Rose exclaimed.

"I know!" Leah said, beaming.

"I assume you want to go?!"

"Of course! Can I? Can I?" she asked excitedly, like she was a little child again.

"But...?" Rose asked, looking at Leah's face as if she was troubled.

"It's **soooo** long away! I'm not sure I can wait that long!"

"I think it's worth the wait!" Rose said, winking.

Also available

Leah and the Football Dragons

There are all kinds of dragons. There are successful dragons who always win and sit on their piles of gold. And then there are the Deadtail Dragons, a boys' football team who know only of defeat.

There is only one talented footballer who can change the fortunes of the Deadtail Dragons. And there is just one problem. That footballer is a girl.

How can Leah win when her local football teams only accept boys? How can she succeed when they tell her that 'Girls can't play football'?

Taking her own destiny in her hands Leah comes up with a bold plan to both fulfil her sporting dreams and help the Deadtail Dragons to fly.

Leah and the Football Dragons is a story for children aged 8 upwards.

www.paulmullinsauthor.co.uk

Made in the USA
Charleston, SC
11 November 2015